CHEW

BY NAOMI AULT

SEASON ONE

Naomi
AULT

ISBN: 979-8-9859726-0-3

For Jim.

Introduction

Chew is a multiseason serial on Amazon's Kindle Vella and is currently publishing on a twice a week basis. Once you complete this book, you can pre-order the next bundle of episodes in paperback or eBook format, or head directly to Kindle Vella by typing this URL into any browser: ReadChew.Live

Chew contains themes and content which may be triggering to some readers. If you'd like to review a list of trigger warnings prior to reading this book, please visit my website at https://www.naomiault.com

Season One

1

Remain Calm

Remain Calm

The first thing you remember is the pain—every nerve in your body exploding all at once. The second thing you remember is your mother. She looked at you in a way she never had before, terrified and pushing you away from her. You grabbed her to hold on to because—Mom, I'm scared—but when you opened your mouth to speak, you bit her. And then you kept biting her. You remember the taste of her blood. The texture of her flesh. The mouthfeel of the two together.

You vomited a lot in the beginning. That's normal in Recovery, they say.

You don't know how long you were an Infected, but you remember a surprising amount about it, which brings you to the third thing. The nightmare thing. The thing that, when the lights are out and everything is still and quiet, you hear all over again—the unrelenting sound of chewing.

You have been saved.

The scientists tell you later that chewing is the only thing that eases the excruciating pain. They explain, while casually standing over you with a circular bone saw, that the act of chewing released a chemical in your brain that neutralized the prion activity, but the pain relief only lasted for as long as you kept chewing. They named the prion Wormwood, which you hate—but not as much as you hate the bone saw—because it conjures images of worms wriggling their way around your brain.

Initially, no one understood what was happening or why. Some people blamed aliens. Some blamed God. Some blamed the Chinese, which always made you wonder who the Republic of China blamed. You?

Follow the instructions given to you.

Anyway, once the prions began activating, everyone was supposed to stay home alone while the government tried to figure out what was happening. Most people experienced a bad flu. Other people felt perfectly fine. Then people started going crazy. They attacked others and ate them like an elegant tartare to be paired with something dry with pleasantly floral undertones.

You've just described your mother's favorite wine, which is what you brought to dinner that day. It was her birthday, and she was sick with worry over your brother because New York City had gone dark the day before. So, you ignored quarantine because, well, poor Mom, but you felt fine. This was important. You were perfectly fine. You'd never have gone if you weren't.

Do not try to leave.

Your father was there when you turned. One second you were eating cake, and then he was asking if you were okay, and then he was screaming at you to step back. Your father escaped, leaving you alone with your mother.

Whom you chewed. You chewed until there was nothing left of her but blood and bone. You were cracking open those bones and trying to suck out the marrow when they found you.

But enough about that. Congrats—you got saved. You don't remember receiving the cure, but you remember waking up one day without pain. They had you strapped down to a bed with something hard stuffed in your mouth between your teeth. A female computer voice told you over a loudspeaker to remain calm, follow directions, and recited platitudes about anger and stuff on a loop. You couldn't tell anyone you were awake or that you were you again. It was hard to cry. Or throw up. That last thing finally brought someone over; when the vomit aspirated into your lungs, making some alarm go off, forcing someone to go through the trouble of saving you all over again. You wish you knew who, so you could hate them personally.

To avoid relapse, manage your emotions appropriately.
Sadness serves no purpose.
Anger is pointless.
Fear is unproductive.
Laughter can be dangerous.

The cure isn't a guarantee. It is impossible to tell who has a chance of surviving the treatment, so the army shoots tranquilizer darts at any Infected they come across that don't look too physically damaged. For many Infected, the cure is just a quiet and pain-free death—strapped to gurneys they never get up from again. Not you, though. Eventually, they get you up off that gurney and lead you outside to a giant open yard surrounded by armed soldiers and razor wire. They fire-hose the muck off you and toss you a mostly dry bright-orange jumpsuit to put on afterwards.

While violent shivers rack through you, courtesy of your nighttime outdoor shower, you watch as they wheel out the ones who never woke up. They dump them and burn them in a pit close to the yard. They want you to see, you know. The soldiers saved you because they were told to, not because they wanted to. You can tell by the way they cling to their guns and how they never look you in the eye. Eventually, people show up outside the yard with protest signs and angry faces and shout at you to die through the fence.

If only, you think.

Eventually, and probably because of the attention you're getting from the people outside the fence, they build an indoor facility. When they move everyone, you're fitted with an anti-bite device that looks like a mask, and they brand you with the letter I on your upper arm, marking you as Infected. The soldier who holds the brand is the first Normal to look you in the eye since you've been here. He apologizes and tells you it's going to hurt. You smell burnt flesh, but you don't tell him it doesn't hurt or that he doesn't know what pain really is because you don't want to scare him away. He's not your friend, but he is the first and only Uninfected human who isn't immediately your enemy.

Scientists come and go. They fit a strange sort of screw tab for the hole in your skull. Researchers need to constantly analyze the fluid that your brain stews in, they explain, and this is less intrusive. They never ask you if having a permanent hole in your head feels less intrusive to you.

They hurt you on purpose; they need to know if you can still feel pain and what your response is. Biters hurt each other, too, and the people in charge just watch with clipboards in their hands. They try to anger you and make you sad. They explain that your feelings could trigger a relapse, and they need to be sure before letting you go.

You have no rights. You have no voice. You are not human. You're Infected. A Biter, if you want to be politically incorrect. Because of this, and in the interest of science, they've done unimaginable things to you, but this is the first time you've been truly scared of them—*let you go?*

Your nightmares immediately take a new turn. Now the throng of Uninfected is attacking and eating you, instead of the other way around.

One day, the regularity of experimentation dies down, which makes you suspicious. Either they are going to finally make good on their threat to turn you out into the world again, or they've decided you are of no value whatsoever. At night, when you're trying to stay awake for as long as possible, so you don't dream, you're not sure which outcome you should root for.

They start a program that involves you and another Biter sitting face-to-face to practice talking about the weather. Not everyone can do that; the Droolers and the Mumblers sure can't, and the pit—which has been silent for weeks—fires up for one brief afternoon. They begin to serve solid food in the cafeteria, and you lose ten pounds before they take you away and stuff a feeding tube down your throat.

"You have to eat," you're told. They expect you to *chew*? You lie and say you'll do better, but you mostly do better at pretending. Your waistband says you are fifteen pounds down by the time they take away slippers and issue everyone a nice fresh pair of shoes. You recognize the brand on sight, but the logo is missing because you're so vile that a soulless corporation doesn't want to be associated with your feet. Man, that makes you and the others laugh in the yard. You laugh and laugh and laugh.

The army started packing while you were sleeping. The yard is gone, the pit filled in, and the fences taken down. It's like it never happened. All that's left is the temporary shelter they housed you in, and they start taking it down before they even usher you out of the building. They line you up and hand each of you a small manila envelope containing exactly ninety-nine dollars in cash and a paper with laws on it, recently passed by Congress, while the country is still under martial law.

Ten Laws of the United States of America and the Emergency Unified Congress Governing all Prion-Infected Humans (Infected) In force October 25, 2019

1. In the interest of public safety, all Infected must wear their government-issued anti-bite device at all times while they are in the presence of an Uninfected citizen, under punishment of death.
2. No Infected will own or possess a firearm, under penalty of death.
3. No Infected shall gather in numbers greater than four, under penalty of death.
4. No Infected may remove or alter their mark in any way, under punishment of death.
5. All Infected must report to a Recovery Center at the frequency mandated by local or state government, without

exception, under punishment of imprisonment. Repeated violations will incur the death penalty.

6. No Infected may reside further than thirty minutes' walking distance from a Recovery Center, under punishment of imprisonment. Repeated violations will incur the death penalty.

7. All Infected must contribute to the economy. No Infected will turn down assigned work or suitable employment, under punishment of imprisonment. Repeated violations will incur the death penalty.

8. No Infected shall engage in sexual relations with an Uninfected citizen, under punishment of death.

9. No Infected shall conceive a child unless approved by a qualified scientist in a Recovery Center. Failure to obtain proper written approval will result in forfeiture of the child and possible imprisonment for violators.

10. All Infected must manage their emotions appropriately, as taught in Recovery. If an Infected is feeling excessive emotion, they should isolate themselves immediately and call 911. State immediately that you have a Relapse Emergency and wait for further instructions with your government-issued anti-bite device securely in place.

God Bless the United States of America

You're one of the last to leave, and by the time they shuffle you out the door, the entire group of Biters is standing in the middle of the desert with no idea what to do next. They dismantle the last of the center while you all watch and whisper to each other about it. It's all wholly erased; you can't even tell where the bodies are buried. If you ever wanted to come back someday, there isn't a single thing to gawk at and feel tortured about. All the twisted mementos of your time there will have to exist solely in your head.

And they do.

The last of the staff drive away in the packed truck. They just leave you there. No water. No food. No idea where you even are.

It's fucking unbelievable, is what it is.

They mentioned that your surviving family, the ones you listed on a form somewhere in the beginning, were notified about your release and invited to greet and collect you. No one shows up. You try not to be disappointed; after all, you have no idea if your family is even still alive. Your brother could be in Recovery just like you, although you hope he isn't. You hope he died outright or made it through unscathed. You don't want this for him; he deserves better.

Not all of you make it. But that's the way it's been since you got cured, right? Not everyone survived the cure; not everyone survived the yard, and not everyone survived talking 'bout the fuckin' weather. It only makes sense that not everyone will survive being let go. Christ, you don't even have a shovel to bury them. You're forced to leave them like ghoulish guideposts throughout the desert.

Civilization is waiting for you; the mob is angry and wild. They don't want you there, and they illustrate this point with guns, knives, and bats.

The girl is maybe fifteen years old. You stand over her as her rail-thin, emaciated body twitches on the ground. Red blood pools under her head and makes a halo around her blond hair. The guy who killed her stands across from you. He grips the murder weapon in one hand, a baseball bat, and regards his handiwork with a smug, satisfied look on his face.

Before she dies, you make eye contact with her. You're the very last person she ever sees. She survived so much, and—well, it only takes a second before the sadness hurts. It starts in your heart and then spreads like wildfire.

You leap over her body at him; he's so surprised that he doesn't react fast enough to throw you off. You have him pinned to the ground. He screams for help while he desperately tries to reach the bat that he dropped, but it rolled too far away.

You tell him what you learned in the Recovery Center. "Remain calm."

And then you chew.

2

Magic Man

ALLISON ROSE

Temporary Recovery Center | Cincinnati, Ohio
October 1, 2019
244 days post-WPE (Wormwood Prion Event)

They met in the yard, up against a chain-link fence, mud tugging at their shoes. Thick black smoke billowed from the pit where the soldiers were burning the bodies. A timely gale swept the ashy plumes in their direction, framing them against a raw pewter sky.

Allison wasn't sure how long he'd been watching her, but the moment she realized he was, she stole a spoon during her kitchen shift and sharpened the handle. By the time of their meeting, which he would later describe as ordained by Heaven, her small piece of gleaming stainless steel was ready for service.

Without ever actually touching her, he used his body to force her backwards until her spine pressed against the fence at the rear of the yard, the stinking pit smoldering in the field fifty yards behind her. They were alone. No one ever went back there during body disposal unless they wanted to do something that they didn't want an audience for.

He looked to be at least ten years older than her; crow's feet around his eyes gave him away. He was taller than her but not remarkably so, maybe 5'11" if she had to give a description. Not that she'd have to—no one in charge concerned themselves with what Biters did to each other.

They had shaved his head during intake just like everybody else, but his hair had grown about a fingertip's length, coming in sandy blond and hinting that it might be wavy once it really got going. The smoke stung his hazel eyes and gave them an edge of crimson, but his teeth were fully funded, 401(k) straight when he grinned and introduced himself. "I'm Will. Will Taylor."

He reminded her of a shark. "I've been watching you."

"Is that right?" she asked while she coaxed the shank down her sleeve without him noticing. Before she was cured, Allison had been both young and pretty, so it was not the first time that a man had come into her space uninvited. But once she worked the bowl of the spoon down into her palm, she'd wrap her fingers around nice and tight and make good ole boy Will Taylor the last to grin and get away with it.

She gave him a smile and hoped it looked sincere. "I'm Al."

"I know that." He hooked his fingers in the fence behind her, and leaned down, his face just inches from hers. "I make it my business to know all kinds of things. For instance, I know that the kid isn't yours."

"So what?"

"I know that you get nightmares just like everybody else, but you don't cry after." Will's hand dropped from the fence; he grabbed her wrist and squeezed it just hard enough to make his next point. "And I know that you've got a shank in this here sleeve with my name on it because you know I've been watching you."

She tried to pull her wrist free, to test his strength, but he was bigger and stronger. Her survival had depended on him not knowing about the weapon.

Allison had quit believing in God shortly after her brother's third overdose—something about the sight of him in the hospital bed, all skin and bones and scratching at himself, writhing to leave so he could get high all over again, had soured her on the concept of intelligent design. Sometimes though, out of the habit of a good Catholic upbringing, she prayed for things for other people. At that moment, pinned by a large man against a fence in a place too similar to Hell to be anything but, she asked God for the kid's checkup to take longer than normal. She asked God not to let the kid see what he was about to do to her.

Will snickered. "I'm not gonna touch you, Al."

He let go of her and stepped back, giving her about three feet of breathing room. "I needed to see what you'd do if you thought I was going to."

The unexpected turn left Allison speechless. He seemed content to wait until she had something to say about it. "What if I had been quicker and stabbed you?"

He shrugged that unimportant detail away. "I had to make sure that I was right about you. See how you acted when your back was against the wall. The smiling thing you did there was a nice touch."

Allison gripped the shank firmly. "Thanks."

"There aren't many like us, Al. Not in here. Maybe not anywhere."

"Like us?"

"You and me are the same. I get you. For instance, that kid. See, other people look at her and they think she's just deadweight for you. You're doing some kind of charity by taking care of her." He squinted. "But that's not how it is, is it?"

Allison found herself drawn in. "How is it?"

"There's a lot swirling around in here when we wake up." Will pointed to his head. "But you, you wake up and vomit all over yourself just like the rest of us, but instead of rolling over and wishing you'd died, or slitting your wrists in the canteen like that squinty Russian did yesterday, you just get up and find a reason to keep living. That kid's not charity. That kid gives you a reason to live."

He was close. The kid had found Allison, not the other way around. Came out of nowhere and latched right on to Allison's leg right after her awakening, like a daisy-chain-wearing jellyfish. But the rest was pretty spot-on.

He went on. "I want people like you. Someone I can trust."

"And you're sure you can trust me? Ten seconds ago I was gonna stab you, and honestly? I'm still kind of undecided about it," Allison said.

If a smile was anything to go by, Will found the concept of being stabbed very agreeable. "Where at?"

"Where what?"

"Where were you gonna stab me at?" With his arms out, he turned around in a slow circle and gave her carte blanche over his entire body.

"Well, if you hadn't caught me, I was gonna stick you right in the neck," Allison admitted.

He nodded his approval. "Aggressive. Bold. But my advice is to go for the renal artery by the kidney." He twisted his upper body slightly to show her exactly where he meant. "By the time anybody notices, you're long gone. But make sure you yank the shank back out, so it isn't plugging the hole."

"Thanks, but messy was the point. I needed lots of blood and for everyone to see and know it was me."

He regarded her thoughtfully. "Hmm... that's smart, too. Keep the wolves off you a little while longer. Well, keep in mind I have associates and they might have not taken kindly to my demise. Covert might have been the better play in that situation. If you're looking to make an example out of someone, a loner would probably be best, to avoid any unpleasant retaliation. Anyway, just some friendly free advice."

"Is that what we are? Friends?"

"We could be," he said.

Allison pulled a face.

"Not *that* kind of friend, Al," he said. "And if we were friends, I'd make sure nobody else tried to make you that kind of friend, either."

"Why would you do that?"

"I told you." Will pinched the bridge of his nose in exasperation before going on. "I want someone I can trust. We're not going to be here forever. They're gonna let us go, and then what?"

Allison couldn't help it—she laughed in his face. She realized her error too late, and they froze, waiting to see if she'd been heard by the soldiers. After several tense seconds ticked by, and it seemed they were in the clear, Will grinned. "You don't think so?"

"No, I don't think so." Allison said. "As soon as they're done experimenting on us to save the rest of the world, we're going to end up in that pit back there. I heard they cut the whole top of the Biters' skulls off out in Nevada. I bet they do that to us next."

"If you think that, then why do you look after the kid?" he countered. "Why are you trying to get her to talk? Why tuck her in and tell her bedtime stories? What's the point?"

Allison didn't have an answer for that. She wasn't sure why she got herself out of bed in the morning, let alone anyone else.

"How about this?" Will said. "We'll be friends. One-sided friends. I'll watch after you like I said, and you don't have to do anything in return."

Allison put her hands on her hips. "Do you think I'm stupid?"

"I mean it," Will said. "And if you're right, and we both just end up in the pit, then at least you went... unmolested."

"And if you're right, and they let us go?"

Will smirked. "If I'm right, then you'll work for me. I ask, you do. Unquestioned loyalty at all times. I've got big plans. But I need people I can trust to help make them happen."

"What sort of plans?"

"Sorry, I only share my hopes and dreams with my friends."

Will wasn't the first man she'd caught watching her. She'd planned to make an example out of him and hoped to buy herself some time from the rest—but there was one wiry, squirrelly-looking man who had begun to cast furtive glances at the kid, too. Allison was tired of sleeping with one eye open all the time, and it wouldn't be the worst thing to have friends she could count on to allow her to get a couple hours of proper sleep. Still, she hesitated.

"I'll tell you what." Will sensed her reluctance. "I'm going to tell you a secret. One that I have not uttered to another soul."

"You're going to tell me, who you just met, your deepest, darkest secret?"

"I am," Will said. "You ready?"

Allison had a hard time imagining what he could say that would make her trust him. "Hit me."

Will leaned forward, curved his fingers into the fence just above her ears again, and whispered five words to her. When he finished speaking, Allison couldn't bring herself to look him in the eye. "Yep, just like I thought."

Allison put her shiv away. Over the years, skepticism had fastened itself to her personality, but with just five simple words,

Will had won her over. Thus began a dance that they would perform many times over, for the remainder of their friendship.

He uncurled his fingers from the fence and stepped back. He cocked his head when he asked, "What did you do before this?"

"I was a cook," Allison said. "I worked at a diner in Cincinnati. Well, two diners, actually. And on Mondays I was a cashier at the mall."

"Excellent! I like my eggs over easy," he informed her.

"Well, I don't know why you're telling me that. I ain't ever making you breakfast," Allison said.

He linked her arm through his and escorted her to the main concourse, as if it were prom and not a muddy yard surrounded by razor wire, tanks, and black smoke.

"Sure you will. But first we're going to need a kitchen and some eggs."

3

Charlie With the Eight Toes

Cincinnati, Ohio
December 27, 2019
331 days post-WPE

A llison had fond memories of her grandmother, who she called Gamma. She spent several weeks at Gamma's every summer, and while she recalled little of her childhood, she remembered those precious summer weeks very well. Allison frequently had to rely on her memories of Gamma to figure out how to care for Kid.

Kid didn't communicate, nor did she seem likely to, so learning her name was impossible. Faced with the need to call her something, she decided to call her Kid until the girl could tell Allison what her proper name was. Allison had convinced herself that Kid previously enjoyed a happy life, which included a large and loving family. Choosing a new name for Kid seemed to Allison like she was trying to erase the child's old life.

It was with Gamma in mind that they spent many days on Allison's bunk, with Allison sitting behind Kid, brushing her hair, and humming a song that she couldn't recall the lyrics to. While there, Allison could almost forget they were smack dab in the middle of a room full of refugees: some perpetually sad, some perpetually angry, and some who just didn't feel anything at all. They carried on around Allison and Kid, and her bunk was a life preserver in a sea of trauma that would devour them, in some form or another, if Allison let it.

One rainy day, while Allison was brushing Kid's hair and had nearly hummed herself into a light trance, Will came up and leaned against the bunk over hers with his back to her. His gait was still jerky and stilted from his follow-up testing the day before, though he was trying hard to hide it. His hand slipped out of his pocket, and he held it out behind him, palm up. "Hey, I need that present you made for me."

Allison removed the homemade shiv from her sock and laid it in Will's palm.

Without looking at her, he said, "Grab your stuff and take Kid over to my bunk. Capiche?"

"Why?"

"You know that guy, Charlie, with the eight toes?"

Charlie Sonchecka had eight toes but twenty friends by Allison's last count. "Yeah."

"He recruited that rat-face guy this morning to do a job. You know who he is, Peddo-Freddo."

She knew exactly who he was. Peddo-Freddo was the main reason she'd taken Will up on his offer to be friends in the first place. He used to try to hide his longings, but lately he'd become brazen and stared at Kid openly. Allison's heart pounded in her chest while she shoved her meager belongings into a pillowcase. "To do what?"

"Doesn't matter. What matters is how Charlie plans to pay Freddo."

Allison jumped off her bunk, Kid's hand gripped tightly in hers. Charlie, Peddo-Freddo, and three of Charlie's guys were walking in their direction.

"What are you going to do?"

Will grinned around his well-gnawed toothpick. "You'll see in a minute. But from my bunk. If things go sideways, you stall like we talked about. You do whatever you have to. Get going."

Allison swallowed hard and lifted Kid up with one arm while she carried the pillowcase containing their worldly goods in her other hand. Balancing Kid on her hip, she briskly made her way through the maze of bunks to Will's, which was on the far end of the dormitory, against a wall. She glanced behind her; Will and Charlie were talking, but Freddo's eyes fixated on her and Kid. Allison picked up the pace.

She knew the minute the fighting broke out without the need to look behind her. The rain had kept everybody out of the yard and inside the building, so the moment that one of the men started swinging, all the Biters were on hand to witness it. They leaped from their cots, hungry for a spectacle to break the tedium of the day. Will had a modest crew loyal to him, and the ones not already at his side shoved past Allison on their way to back him up. One stepped on her foot in his rush to get to Will, causing her to stumble a little, before regaining her balance. Half limping, Allison reached Will's bunk and boosted Kid up to the top, and then she scrambled up after.

From there, she had a better view of the action. Will was still on two feet, but Charlie was on the ground, writhing and bleeding like a stuck pig. She didn't see Freddo at first, but found him when she scanned the crowd—he'd slipped away from Will and was heading through the crowd of eager onlookers, straight towards her.

Allison had nothing to defend herself with, but Freddo was going to have to climb up to them, so she pushed Kid against the wall and put herself between the child and Freddo. She braced her position by grabbing the rail at the head of the bed and got ready to start kicking.

Her first kick was well-placed, and Freddo fell to the floor, holding his head and looking dazed. He got back up slowly, shaking his head as if to clear it. His next approach was more cautious—he tried to grab her feet, intending to hold her still. Allison kicked at him as hard and fast as she could. His hand connected with her ankle, but she yanked her leg back and slipped from his grasp.

She kicked again, landing a lucky blow to his face. He fell back down to the floor with a thud. At his whiny cries, she peeked over the side of the bed. Freddo held his nose and rolled back and forth on the floor. Blood seeped out from under his hand and dripped down his face.

He had a tinny, annoying voice on a good day, and the broken nose didn't improve upon it. He stood up, called Allison a bitch in a high-pitched squeal, and made another grab at her. She pushed back from the edge of the bed and kicked at him but didn't connect. His hand wrapped around her ankle, but she slipped out of his grasp, his digits too bloody to hold on to her.

Her next kick missed again, and he grabbed her once more. This time, his fingers burrowed down into her ankle and anchored there. She couldn't get free. She kicked at him with her other foot, but he pulled himself up and used his body weight to hold both her legs down.

He was on top of her, his greasy, pockmarked face beaming in victory. His nose dripped blood onto her face. She turned her head away from him to avoid it, but warm drops fell on her cheek and into her ear.

"I'm going to kill you," he breathed. He put a hand on her chin and turned her face and looked her in the eye. "And then I'll take what's mine."

Their faces were close enough that she could have bitten him. The idea of it turned her stomach, but she was weaponless and immobilized. She was about to close her eyes and do the deed when a thought hit her: if a doctor or a soldier was watching, and saw her biting him, they'd shoot her for relapse. They would probably shoot Freddo, in case the relapse spread, which was a plus, but they might shoot Kid, too, to be thorough.

Freddo breathed directly into her face. He stunk like rotted garbage. "Maybe she wants to go with me. You ever think of that?"

Allison wriggled and bucked, shifting him enough to get her knee up under his nuts, and she jerked her leg up, hard and fast. The maneuver rewarded her with another of his high-pitched squeals of pain. She bucked again and used her arms to push him as hard as she could, dislodged him enough to get a leg free, and pushed him off her. He disappeared over the edge of the bunk.

She peered over the edge in time to see Will kneeling over Freddo, Allison's homemade shiv buried in his throat. Will yanked it back out, blood spraying across his chest and face, but Will stabbed him again, for good measure. He pulled the shiv out and wiped it off on the leg of his jumpsuit before standing back up and slipping the shiv into his pocket.

She noticed Will's hand had a slight tremor that wasn't there the day before, and he was favoring his ribs.

"Is he dead?" Allison asked, climbing down to join him.

"Is he—is he *dead*?" Will asked. "Well, let's ask him. Hey, Peddo-Freddo, are you dead?"

There was a gurgling sound; the air escaping Freddo's throat pushed bubbles up through the gushing blood. Then nothing.

Across the room, a cluster of scientists furiously scribbled on clipboards—except for one. Will had bestowed the moniker of Doctor Harpy on the lone nonscribbling scientist, explaining that harpies tortured souls on their way down to Hell. Allison thought the nickname suited the doctor perfectly. Doctor Harpy motioned for soldiers to enter the dorm and start clearing away the carnage.

When they got to Freddo's body, one of them gave Will a questioning look.

He shrugged. "I don't know, boss. He just fell over like that."

Accustomed to Will's personality, the two soldiers shook their heads and carried Freddo away. Will went to the latrine and cleaned himself up. When he came back, he sat down next to Allison and Kid on the lower bunk. "Charlie's boys are going to be sore for a while about this. I'm taking this bunk, and you're staying up top from now on."

Allison didn't argue. "Thanks."

Will nodded and draped an arm around his ribs. "Yeah. Yeah. Get out of my luxury suite so I can lie down and catch my breath."

"Why?"

"Because that fucking Russian kicked the shit out of me. God damn, he had strong feet."

"No, I mean, why are you protecting us?"

"We covered this already. Remember? In the yard."

"Yeah, but—"

"Why do you protect Kid?"

Doctor Harpy, during one of her intense head-shrinking sessions, had told Allison she'd attached to Kid because her chewing routinely flooded her brain with something called oxytocin, the same brain chemical that caused mothers to become attached to their newborn babies, and it had still been floating around in her brain when she woke up and met Kid.

"You don't love her," Doctor Harpy had explained. "Your brain just tricked you into getting attached to her."

Allison found the explanation hard to believe. She felt something for Kid, and while she couldn't tell if it was love or not, it was strong—they were connected. She opened her mouth to explain it to Will, but nothing would come out.

"Ditto," Will stated. He pointed up to the bunk above him.

Allison and Kid climbed up and left Will to recover from his injuries.

"Will?" Allison whispered down.

"What?"

"What's the big plan you keep talking about?"

A huffy sigh drifted up to her. "You really need to know right now?"

It had been several months since she'd met him, and he'd hedged every time she tried to ask. "Yes."

"Fine." He winced. "They're gonna let us all go. And when they do, we're going to need our own place."

"Can't everyone just go back to our families? I mean, the ones that still have them."

"How many letters from family do you see coming in here? How many family visits have you heard of?"

Will had a point. There was never any mail except court summons. Bills apparently still had to be paid, and the Biters not paying them were losing tangible property and assets like water in a sieve. She didn't know of anyone getting called down to the family visiting room, which was supposed to happen twice a month.

"I guess I wasn't paying attention because I don't have anyone to visit me."

"Me either."

There were several minutes of silence from both bunks.

"So you're going to start a place for us all to go?" Allison whispered down.

"We are. And it will be better if I show you, instead of telling you. But you'll see. Don't worry."

Something occurred to Allison. "Have *you* seen it?"

She listened to his labored, shallow breathing below. It was several minutes before he responded. "Yes. When I woke up that first time, just for a second. I saw some other stuff, too. But I saw our home. And it was like... well, my words can't do it justice."

Allison had heard a few other Biters talking about visions during their "awakening," as some of them called it. She was surprised that Will had seen one, and even more surprised to discover he believed in it.

"Didn't you see anything when you woke up?" he asked her.

"Not that I can remember. I just remember throwing up and wanting to get up right away. Like I had something to do or somewhere to be. Imagine my surprise that I wasn't about to go anywhere."

He laughed. "I was there."

"You were?"

"You cost me twelve pudding packs that day. I bet against you."

"You did? Why?" she asked, indignant.

"Because I didn't recognize you."

"What does that mean?"

"It means..." He winced again. "I need to shut my eyes a bit."

Allison became silent so Will could get some rest. From her new perch on the top bunk, Allison could see the whole floor. The big fight was already forgotten, and the Biters had gone back to the business of doing nothing. She assumed Will had fallen sleep, but about twenty minutes later, a very wide-awake-sounding Will called up to her. "Hey, Al?"

"Yeah?"

"I got pulled for a follow-up yesterday."

She thought about the tremor in his hand and the weird jerk in his step. She leaned her head over the side, and looked at him while hanging upside down. "I know."

"Saw a couple white-coats exchangin' gifts while I was back there."

"So?"

"Well, they were wrapped in Christmas paper."

"Is it Christmas?"

"Might be. Or close to it." He was quiet for a moment, and then he reached in his pocket and pulled out the still bloody shiv. He held it up for her to take it back.

Allison took it, curled up with Kid on the top bunk, and fell asleep with it in her hand.

4

Every Casino in Vegas

Cincinnati, Ohio
February 28, 2020
394 days post-WPE

W ill traded a guy named Dave Smalls a lighter for a deck of cards. The lighter was contraband of the highest order. Will only had it because he never turned down the opportunity to own something of value, but he was glad to unload it in exchange for something less dangerous and more entertaining. Dave Smalls got caught three days later trying to burn down the entire building, and there was an investigation about where the lighter had come from, but luckily Dave was an arsonist and not a snitch.

Upon discovering that Allison had never played poker, Will made her his pupil. He started with Five-Card Stud and then moved on to Texas Hold 'Em. It was during this instruction that he recognized two things about Allison: she was a fast learner where sums and numbers were concerned, and she was probably dyslexic. To his mind, she was perfect.

Allison became adept at the mechanics of poker, but much less so at the art of bluffing. In an effort to teach her about misdirection, he'd engaged her in a heated disagreement about whether ketchup belonged on steak, when something seized his attention. He fidgeted with the toothpick in his mouth and motioned for Allison to look behind her. Soldiers were wheeling in large carts and arranging them next to long tables. Because they had been guests of the army long enough to recognize what processing looked like, Allison grabbed Kid's hand out of reflex.

The loudspeakers, which had consistently played a mantra of state-approved platitudes, went silent, and the effect was stunning. Every Biter in the room froze and shifted their attention to the only sound in the room: the squeaking of table legs across hard floors.

The abrupt change in the routine prompted Kid to plaster herself to Allison's waist. If the army planned for them to be separated, they would need to fetch one of their tanks to blast the child loose. After several minutes of silence, the loudspeakers came back online with fresh directives. They were to line up, in any order they pleased, and wait for their turn. What they were lining up for was suspiciously absent from the directions. Will arranged for them to be in front of him in the line—his vow in the yard to watch her back was something he'd taken in the most literal sense.

Will leaned forward and whispered, "Just like I said."

"You think they're letting us go?"

"No point setting all this up if they're just going to shoot us and dump us into a pit," Will said.

There was a particular logic in that, and Allison smoothed Kid's hair, an absentminded gesture that calmed them both. Will generally kept his distance from Kid, citing a lack of enthusiasm for small children. He doled out nuggets of advice here and there, and he made sure Kid had enough to eat because, he said, it mattered to Allison, but beyond that Allison was on her own. Will glanced at Allison, who was comforting Kid, and fiddled his toothpick a little more vigorously than before, but said nothing.

Hopeful anticipation and dread weighed equally on Allison as they inched ahead. Once they got closer to the front of the line, Allison could hear what the soldiers were telling the Biters at the front of the lines.

"This is a stipend from the government. You have seventy-two hours to report and register with a Recovery Center. Here is a list of established sites."

"These are the Ten Laws for the Infected."

"You are required to work no less than twenty-five hours per week in a government-directed work program."

"Sign here."

Allison whispered over her shoulder. "Holy shit, Will. I think you're right."

"I'm going to choose not to be offended that you had any doubt," Will said.

When it was Allison and Kid's turn, she helped Kid hold a pen in her hand and make an "X" for her name. She took the envelopes for herself and Kid and received the same spiel that everyone else had received. They each got a swift injection in the arm. When it was time to sign the work program papers, she paused.

"What about her?" Allison pointed at Kid, whose death grip on Allison's leg was giving her foot the tingles.

"What about her?"

"She's like... seven years old. You want her to get a job?" Allison asked.

"That's the law," the soldier answered. "Sign here."

Allison did not sign there. "What is a seven-year-old girl going to do, exactly?"

Will stepped up and set his hand on her shoulder. The armed soldier next to the processing table put his hand on his rifle around the same time Will spoke in a low voice. "Let's not look a gift horse in the mouth."

Allison signed the paper and moved on.

"Listen, you need to learn when to pick your battles," Will lectured her outside later. A gusty wind blew his hair around, and he ran a hand through it to tame it back down. "Not everything is a hill to die on."

It was brisk, but the air was missing the distinctive bite of January, and there was less than an inch of dirty old snow on the ground. Allison had lived in Ohio her entire life and calculated it to be February, maybe even the very early days of March. She pulled out the list of Recovery Centers. There was one in Cincinnati, but it was going to be a lengthy trek, and they wore jackets designed for brief periods in the yard, not extended trips in the cold. The metal from the anti-bite mask lay flush against her cheeks and nose, her skin already stinging from the cold contact.

"You smell that?"

Allison sniffed. She smelled all sorts of things on the wind, and she wasn't sure specifically which one Will was referring to. "Smell what?"

"Freedom." He stretched out his arms, prepared to embrace the open sky. After a few moments, he dropped his arms to his sides and got down to business. "First thing we gotta do is get to Pittsburgh."

"I don't even know how we're getting to Cincinnati without freezing to death, and you want to go hours away to Pittsburgh?" Allison asked. The injection site on her arm smarted, and she held it up to Will to remind him that they had trackers implanted in them. "And the clock's ticking. We only got seventy-two hours to check in with a permanent Recovery Center."

"Well, we have to go to Pittsburgh first. I got something stashed there, and then we'll be set." Will rubbed his hands together. Allison wasn't sure if he was doing it out of anticipation of retrieving whatever he had stashed in Pittsburgh or if he was trying to warm them.

Kid trembled around Allison's hip. "Forget it. We need to get someplace warm. The sooner, the better."

Will looked inside his small manila envelope; he plucked out stiff green bills and counted them. "Ninety-nine dollars. The *hell* are we supposed to do with—check yours and Kid's."

Allison checked. They had ninety-nine dollars each.

"I'm going to get us someplace warm, and then to Pittsburgh," Will said. "Do you believe me?"

Not wholly, but she nodded.

Will spit out his toothpick, and he sucked on his teeth for several moments before holding out his hand. "Give me yours and Kid's money."

With no place to spend it, the money was worthless paper with precisely as much value as the envelope that held it. But besides the clothes on her back, that money was all she had in the world. Allison handed their cash over and hoped she wasn't mistaken about Will.

"I'll be right back," Will said.

The other Biters realized quickly that they needed to sort out transportation on their own, and they started shuffling down the highway in many directions. Will's posse, the assemblage of men that had followed Will around camp like he was the Messiah, milled around the side of the road. Allison wondered if Will had collected their stipend, too.

The minutes marched on. To pass the time and to suppress her rising anxiety, Allison watched the army tear down the dormitory. She wasn't certain how long she'd been in the Temporary Recovery Center, but judging by the amount her hair had grown back, she supposed it to be around six months. She ran her hand through her hair and wondered what it looked like. There were no mirrors at the center. Not since that one time when a new Biter had woken up, and upon seeing her reflection, smashed the mirror and nearly slit a scientist's throat with one of the shards.

Regardless of the amount of time she'd lived under its roof, the sight of the building being dismantled tugged at her core, and she couldn't articulate why. It should please her to watch it go, given the sinister things that had transpired between its four walls. But then, she mused, she'd come out of it with Kid—someone to freeze to death with while she waited on Will, who had most certainly run off with their meager fortune. Allison knelt down on the pavement, wanting to be eye level with Kid when she lied to her. "I'm gonna figure this out. Okay?"

Kid went on sucking her thumb. Allison wasn't certain if Kid understood Allison when she spoke to her, or if Kid's default setting was blind trust.

Allison stood up and was contemplating her own default setting where Will was concerned, when a semitruck eased onto the highway, pulling away from the partially deconstructed dormitory. Allison noted the direction and determined that she and Kid should start walking the same way, but instead of passing them by, the truck came to a stop. The passenger door opened, and Will's head popped out, a fat grin on his face.

"Going my way?"

Jeremiah Robinson was a drafted private who owed a burly man named Tommy Fingers twenty-five thousand dollars in a transaction conducted before the Prion Event. Jeremiah had hoped the prions would wipe Tommy out, and his debt with him, but Jeremiah was so unlucky that he could not even count on an apocalyptic disease to achieve good fortune.

Jeremiah was not excited to share his cab space with three Biters, but if he didn't pay Tommy at least four thousand dollars by the following day, then Tommy was going to do something unspecified but unpleasant to Jeremiah's girlfriend, a comely girl just shy of seventeen. If Tommy Fingers had threatened Jeremiah's wife, a fresh-faced and unsuspecting woman of thirty, the trio would have likely been walking to Cincinnati like the rest of the Biters. As it was, the seventeen-year-old had captured Jeremiah's lecherous heart, and the fortuitous agreement with Will meant he'd have the payment plus another thousand to feed the slots again that very evening.

Allison was oblivious to all of this: she saw a man in a uniform with a pinched mouth, and a tight jaw, who stared steadfastly at the road ahead of them. Between succumbing to the prion, followed by six months inside of a Recovery Center, Allison had come to live in a state of reactionary survival, and so she paid him no more mind and would continue to do so until Jeremiah did something that warranted her scrutiny. Will positioned himself to sit between their driver and the two girls. Allison took Kid from Will, placed the child in her lap, and tucked Kid's head under her chin. Will put an arm around Allison and pulled them both in against him to help warm them up faster, but it was a while before Allison could stop shaking from the cold and even longer before Kid quit shivering.

"Do you have anything to eat or drink for the little girl?" Will asked Jeremiah after they had been on the road for a while.

Jeremiah shook his head. That was a lie. He had a bottle of soda in his pack, but Kid wasn't old enough, and Allison was too old for Jeremiah's tastes; therefore, he was unlikely to do anything to impress either of them.

Will leaned over and said into Allison's ear, "It's a four-hour drive, but he's got to stop in Columbus and drop this truck off. He's going to take us the rest of the way in his own car. We'll get Kid fed in Pittsburgh."

"He's going to take us to Pittsburgh for three hundred dollars?" Allison asked.

"No, for five thousand dollars," Will said. "The three hundred was a down payment."

She was about to ask where they were going to get that much money, but stopped herself in time so she didn't tip over Will's potential con. She nodded and hoped that if it was a swindle, the soldier was dumb and didn't have an itchy trigger finger. The discussion finished, Will withdrew his arm from Allison's shoulders and scooted a few inches away from her to give them both some breathing room.

Kid was fast asleep when they hit the city limits of Columbus. Jeremiah eased the truck into some sort of depot; there were miles of dump trucks and heavy equipment there. The love-struck, greedy private finally talked to them directly. "You guys hide over there and stay out of sight, so nobody sees those jumpsuits and masks."

The sky deepened to night, and the wind had picked up considerably, giving the early evening air sharp teeth and claws. When Will handed Kid down, she woke up and complained by immediately clutching on to Allison and wrapping her arms and legs around her like a front-facing backpack. Kid was light to carry, which worried Allison because she figured Kid should weigh more. She was always in a constant state of worry about Kid, perpetually believing herself to be a terrible caretaker.

She put her familiar concerns aside for new ones. "I don't think he's coming back."

"He's definitely coming back."

"How can you be so sure?"

"Every casino in Vegas is how."

"What does that mean?"

"Greed, Al. Just simple greed."

"What happens when he asks for the rest of the money?"

Will shrugged. "I'll give it to him."

"You have it?"

"Of course, I have it. I'm not a con man." He threw his shoulders back a little and frowned down at her.

"How much do you have?"

"Enough," he said. "We can afford to toss these orange bull's-eyes we're walking around in and get us some normal clothes and a hot meal."

"The masks are as big of a bull's-eye as the jumpsuits are," Allison pointed out.

"You're right. That's why we're not wearing them once we get to Pittsburgh," Will said.

"That's against the law," Allison argued. "I don't much care about the law so much as I care about the death penalty that they've attached to it."

"I know, but we'll need to blend in, and we can't do that wearing masks, old prison jumpsuits, and these stupid shoes."

Allison was quiet for a few moments. "I like the shoes."

"Me too. They're surprisingly comfortable." Will bounced up and down on the balls of his feet a few times. "But Normals are going to realize that all the Biters are wearing them, so they gotta go."

"What about our arm brands?" Allison asked. "A giant 'I' scar is kind of a dead giveaway, too."

"We don't have enough money for that," Will said. "But it's cold enough that long sleeves won't be out of place. And once we get to where we're going, the brands won't matter anymore."

"And where's that?"

He was still watching for the soldier and didn't look at her to give his cryptic reply. "You'll see."

She changed tactics. "Why us?"

"What?" That got his attention.

"Why me and Kid? You left your crew standing by the side of the road and didn't even say goodbye. Now you're gonna spend five grand on us, plus food and clothes and whatever else it costs to get to wherever we're going. I'd like to know what that's going to cost me, eventually."

His eyes flicked over Allison, and then he resumed his careful watch for their ride. "We covered this. You work for me now. I've got some things to do, and I'd like to have someone with me who isn't likely to stab me in the back while I do it," Will said. "Besides, it was going to cost me that much to get there, anyway. All I'm really out extra is the clothes and food."

That wasn't good enough for Allison. "I ain't never in my life had a man spend a dime on me that wasn't expecting something. Nothing is free. I'm just saying."

He opened his mouth to speak, changed his mind, and closed it. He bit the inside of his cheek, contemplating further before he continued. "Listen. Those other men that you knew before, whoever they were, got nothing to do with the here and now. I haven't lied to you yet. I told you they'd let us go, and they did. Then I told you I'd get us someplace warm and to Pittsburgh, and current temperature notwithstanding, we are halfway to Pittsburgh. I watched your back, and I'm *still* watching your back. I just want you to start watching mine. And that's all I want from you. Ever. Are we friends or not?"

Her voice sounded a little small when she answered him. "Yes, fine. We're friends."

Several minutes of silence passed. Allison interpreted Will's silence as annoyance, but it wasn't. He was wondering, not for the first time, if it was her father or her brother that was the reason she had such a hard time trusting him. He was wrong on both counts; it was her complicated relationship with her mother—a dispassionate woman with a penchant for scratch-off tickets, men with flexible morals, and Pall Malls—that had negatively colored Allison's views on the concepts of trustworthiness and dependability of others.

Allison was not thinking about her mother when she said, "I still don't think he's coming back, though."

Will barked a laugh and rubbed the top of her head. "I don't know why I put up with you."

Will opened the car door, stepped out onto the gravel lot, and crouched down. He wore faded blue jeans and camel-colored boots. His black t-shirt was fresh from the plastic package and still had the factory fold lines on it, long sleeves pushed up to his elbows. The tag scratched the back of his neck when he tilted his head sideways to inspect the dead body from a different angle. He reached back and yanked the offensive tag from the seam before he spoke. "Well, I think you have a great career ahead of you, but you need to work on your technique. You know... try to be a little neater."

Allison's hands were on her knees; she panted hard from the exertion of stabbing a man several times over until he died. Jeremiah Robinson had been her very first murder, and she could not believe how much harder it was in practice than in theory—it had always seemed like it would be easy. She had blood all over her face, neck, and torso—her hands were slick with it. She stood up straight and wiped her hands across her shirt to dry them, leaving huge red streaks across the boobs of her brand-new light-blue hoodie. Once she caught her breath, she defended her performance. "He was about to put your brains all over the inside of the car. I didn't have time to think about how to be neat about it."

Jeremiah had double-crossed them in the end. He'd gotten a whiff of just how much money Will had and figured he could get off Tommy Fingers's books entirely, while waving the rest under his girlfriend's nose. She'd already texted him three times since he'd picked up his car in Columbus, telling him how her mom was working midnights. A fantasy bloomed in his heart and loins: he'd go AWOL and talk her into running away, and they'd have a grand adventure. Not included in his fantasy was her coming up pregnant and eventually aging out of his interest bracket, but if he had survived Allison Rose, that was exactly what would have happened.

Kid made a move to grab hold of her, and Allison barely stepped back in time to avoid her grasp.

"C'mere, Kid," Will intervened. "No sense having to buy both of you new clothes."

Kid climbed up Will and regarded Allison while she sucked her thumb.

Allison tasted salty copper pennies. She spit onto the ground immediately, and frantically tried to wipe her victim's blood away from her mouth by bringing up the collar of her shirt and using it as a napkin. The taste of blood transported her away from the gravel parking lot of the abandoned warehouse building and—

She was in her old trailer in Cincinnati, and her wallet was in her father's liver-spotted hand when she growled and—

Allison coughed and gagged and spit some more until she was standing on gravel again and not on pale green carpet soaked with fresh blood.

Will and Kid seemed to be under some sort of spell that involved staring at the man with the slit throat. "Keys," she said.

She dropped her shiv into her pocket. The souvenir from the Recovery Center had proven handy, and she deftly caught the keys that Will threw at her. She opened the trunk and then began dragging the soldier's body towards it. Once she got it in position, Will called over. "You need any help?"

"No," Allison said. "No sense both of us getting dirty."

Will was oblivious to Allison's sarcasm, so she struggled alone, but after some time and clever leveraging, she got the body into the trunk. Before she shut it, Will and Kid joined her.

"What do we do now?" Will asked her. "Should we take his gun?"

"If we get caught with a gun, it's the death penalty," Allison said.

"This is the death penalty." Will motioned with his head to the dead body in the trunk. "Might as well go all in and take the gun, too. You're pretty good with a knife, looks like, but can't very well bring a knife to every gun fight we find ourselves in."

Jeremiah's face was ghastly white as his blood continued to ooze into a lazy pool at the bottom of the trunk. Will reached in and took the gun. After giving it a practiced once-over, he tucked it comfortably in the back of his pants.

"Should we say something?" he asked.

"What? Like a prayer? I'm the one that killed him in the first place. Ain't that just gonna make God mad?"

Will shrugged.

"You think he had a family?" she asked.

"Maybe," he said. "But maybe not. None of us do. Not anymore."

When Jeremiah didn't show up, that girl would text a boy from school—who would come by and win her heart—blissfully unaware that she'd won a diverted destiny. Jeremiah's wife would never know of Allison directly, but having discovered her husband's affair days before, would thank her every time the widow benefits landed in her bank account. She would meet a kind and honest man a few years later. Jeremiah Robinson was finally a lucky man—just not for himself.

Allison hadn't planned to save a teenager from a predator or make anyone a widow—she had just reacted in defense of Will. She tried to work up some guilt or shame about what she'd done, but it just wouldn't come. She pictured him with a loving wife, and maybe a few kids, but her heart was stone. Instead of remorse, her mind drifted over to the practical matter of covering the car seat, so she didn't get blood on the interior.

At the Center they'd explained a little about the chemicals in their brains, and there was a spiel about hormones, and some other stuff that she couldn't follow like heightened olfactor-something about senses and whatnot. She wished she'd paid better attention or maybe asked some questions, because as she stood there over the body of her very first victim, she found she didn't mind the blood on her at all. It felt, a little bit, like a good fit—maybe even something dangerously close to a perfect fit. She thought, maybe, that she liked it. Jeremiah's murder hadn't moved her one iota, but the idea that she enjoyed killing people made her stomach do a small somersault.

"I think something is wrong with me," she announced to Will.

He looked her over. "You seem fine to me."

"I never killed anyone before being a Biter. What I did when I was a Biter, I mean, I couldn't help that. But this is different," Allison said. "You're not supposed to like killin' people."

Will shook his head and sighed. "Al, first of all, we're still Biters and we're always going to be. All that stuff about recovery at the RC was just a lie to make us feel better about it."

He gave her a sympathetic smile. "Second of all, he was going to kill us. It was simple self-defense. So if it's necessary, what's the big deal if you happen to like it, too?"

She contemplated Will's words carefully. "Will?"

"Yeah."

"I'm watching your back, like you asked."

"I see that. Thank you."

She spit again. "I got his blood in my mouth."

Will closed the trunk, then spoke to her in a tone typically reserved for small children.

"You should probably make sure you close your mouth first next time."

5

Biters Up Ahead

Harmon's Folly, Pennsylvania
February 29, 2020
395 days post-WPE

Will bought Allison clean clothes, and she took a sink-bath in the restroom of a small gas station off of Highway 47. A disinterested clerk with tattoos from fingertip to eyeballs handed her the key, not looking up from his phone when he did so. Allison could hear shrieking and screaming emitting from a tiny speaker and wondered if there was fresh mayhem happening in the world. She didn't know it, but she was only ten miles from the source of that broadcast and would later star in it.

The lavatory was dirty, neglected, and poorly lit. The sink was too shallow for her to fit her head underneath the tap, so she did the best she could to get as much blood out as possible. She stared at herself in the mirror for the first time in almost a year. Her face was much thinner than she remembered, and she had a narrow white scar on her forehead near the hairline—she didn't know where it might have come from. She had a few wrinkles between her eyebrows and around her mouth and eyes. Her skin looked dry and her lips chapped. Her hair hadn't been short, since grade school and with no length to weigh it down, her blond curls were bouncy and wild; however, the residual blood that she couldn't wash out darkened her hair to a shade that she didn't care for.

When she left, she set the key down on the counter. The cashier still didn't look at her, but a bell on the door bid her farewell. Out of spite, Allison flipped the "No Biters" sign around before she let the door go.

With nowhere else to sleep, they spent the night under the roof of Jeremiah's Ford Taurus in a neglected rest stop. Allison worried that she might have a hard time nodding off with a corpse slowly decomposing just a few feet from her in the trunk, but she slept soundly.

Disposing of Jeremiah was a breakfast topic over gas station fare. They had no means to bury him or otherwise conceal the body for any length of time, and if they dumped the body out in the open, it might be discovered quickly, and a hunt would ensue for the killers. After tossing out a few scenarios, they eventually decided they should leave him in the trunk and hide the car. With all the cleanup still in progress, by the time anyone found and towed the car away, they'd be long gone. They drove it a few miles away from the gas station where she'd bathed and changed and hid it just off the road, next to three other abandoned cars—hiding it in plain sight.

Then they walked. They were in rural Pennsylvania, far away from Pittsburgh proper but not quite to the Ohio border. Once they reached Ohio, Will informed her, they would head towards Cleveland.

"What's in Cleveland?"

"Clevelanders." Will kicked a small can in front of him.

"There isn't a Recovery Center in Cleveland," she said.

"I didn't say we were going *to* Cleveland. I just said we were heading towards it," he clarified, kicking the can another few feet ahead of him.

Will, for whatever reason, would not be forthcoming about their ultimate destination, a situation that wasn't as alarming to Allison as it should have been. She wondered if she trusted Will and decided that maybe she did, as much as she could trust anyone. Trust for Allison Rose was a bit like working out a neglected muscle, and she was going to have to practice at it for awhile to get it right.

They journeyed in silence for a time, and the area turned increasingly more rural as they hiked. Allison had never left Ohio before. She had only ever traveled to two places: the neglected small city she was born in, and Cincinnati, where she finished growing up.

Kid was content to walk alongside Allison for a while, but after several miles of looking at double-wides, cornfields, and trees, she began pulling at Allison's shirt to be carried. Allison picked her up and wondered how long she could carry her before her arms gave out. She didn't want to ask Will to help—he'd been pretty clear he didn't want to be involved in the caretaking of Kid, despite some isolated demonstrations of being capable of the task.

She suspected Will had had at least one child before the Flip, but Allison would never inquire outright. Everyone in the Center had lost someone or something when they got infected, and so they had established very early not to ask anyone about their past. It was deemed acceptable to ask about a former occupation, but Will never offered even that much. The closest Will would come to revealing anything about himself to Allison was in the form of a guessing game, which to date, Allison had been unsuccessful at. Allowed just one guess per day, she'd already covered a wide range of professions: businessman, stockbroker, carnie, bull rider and others, but she'd been wrong every time.

Allison was musing her over next guess when she noticed something. "Will? Something's wrong. I smell something kinda... bad."

"Bad like something is rotten? Or bad like you got a bad feeling?"

Allison's stomach turned, and the hair on the back of her neck stood on end. "Both."

Will's game of kick the can stopped at once. He grabbed Allison's arm and walked her into the trees. "Stay here."

Will left her there and went on ahead, following the road, but keeping inside the tree line to stay out of sight of any road traffic. Allison set Kid down to rest her arms, and they sat together under a tree. She figured they might as well rest for as long as they could.

She was getting nervous when, about a half an hour later, Will came back. He was out of breath when he gave her hurried instructions. "We gotta turn around. We can take that side road we saw about a quarter of a mile back. Better if we stay in the trees while we do it."

"What's wrong?" Allison asked, boosting Kid back into her arms and falling in behind Will.

"There're Biters up ahead."

"Isn't that a good thing? We could stay there for the—"

Will stopped and swung around to face her. His face was pale, and he cast furtive glances around them. "No. We can't stay there. We can't stay here. We gotta go."

"Why?"

Will covered up Kid's ears and whispered to her. "I didn't say they were alive."

"They're dead?"

"Some of them. Rest are—they're entertainment, I guess."

"For who?"

Will chewed at the inside of his cheek a bit before grinding out the answer. "Normals. But that's a generous use of the term normal."

"What kind of entertainment?" She had almost not asked, because she dreaded the answer, but curiosity got the better of her.

"The kind we don't need to worry about because we're not going that way. We'll go around." Will's voice was unsteady, shaky. "We should have just kept that fucking car," he cursed to himself under his breath.

While they raced along, Allison remembered the time in the Center when the doctors came and pulled Will out of the chow line, telling him they had some follow-up tests for him. It was well known that many Biters never came back from their follow-up tests, but Will had just patted Allison on the head and nonchalantly told her he'd see her later. He strutted'd across the floor with the doctors as escorts, and loudly flirted with one of them just before disappearing behind the white swinging doors. They did terrible things behind those doors—everyone talked about it. A few weeks after Will's follow-up tests, Allison would get to see for herself.

As she struggled to keep up with Will in the woods, Allison asked herself: if it hadn't scared Will when the doctors pulled him out of line, then *what* had he just seen? Scenarios played out in her mind until she sufficiently spooked herself into a near panic. She picked up the pace and walked alongside, eventually pulling ahead of him.

"Al," he said. She stopped and turned around; he put his hands on both of her shoulders. "Some places are going to be bad, yeah? But not all. We're going to find a good place. We're going to *build* one. I promise. I have a plan. Do you believe me?"

Allison nodded, but her hands were still shaking. She'd had nightmares the last few weeks about being eaten alive by the Normals, and the current turn of events called those nighttime terrors immediately to mind.

Will, ever in tune with Allison's feelings, added, "I haven't let you down yet."

"You haven't," Allison agreed. Reassured, she gave him a terse nod, and Will started leading her through the woods again. Once they got to the road, Will stood for a bit to get his bearings before motioning her to follow him once more. They continued to stay in the tree line, far enough in that they could barely see pavement and hoped passing cars wouldn't be able to see them at all.

"Are we gonna have to sleep out here?" Allison called up to Will's back. She hoped they were far enough away from whatever Will had seen, because her arms were getting tired from carrying Kid. "Because if we are, we should look for a good place soon. We need someplace we can build a fire where nobody will see."

"We can't risk a fire at all, and I'd rather sleep someplace indoors with actual heat."

"Yeah, me too, but I don't see how—"

Allison had been looking at her foot instead of Will and didn't realize that he'd stopped walking until she ran straight into the back of him. She gave a startled "oof." Will's hand snaked around behind his back, and his fingers curled around the handle of the gun they'd stolen. She peeked around Will to see what the matter was.

There was a young man with his back to them, both hands scrambling around the front of his jeans, his knees doing a hurried bounce. His head swiveled back and forth between Will and his business up front. Allison heard the unmistakable sound of a zipper being pulled up.

"Careful," Will said. "Don't want you to hurt yourself there."

"I don't want any trouble," the young man said, turning all the way around and putting his hands up.

He was roughly the same height as Will, with short light-brown hair and black-framed glasses. He wore jeans, and a very faded Ohio State University hoodie that had a story or two to tell.

"That's fantastic," Will said, pulling the gun from his waistband. "Neither do I."

There was a car parked on the road, presumably owned by the man who Will was currently holding at gunpoint. Will motioned for him to head towards it. "Let's take a walk."

He nodded at Will and slowly turned around, keeping his hands high in the air where Will could see them. Will trailed about five paces behind him, and Allison was nearly pressed up against Will's back, holding Kid's hand firmly in her own.

"What's your name?" Will asked.

"Uh—Luke," he said.

"Well, Uh Luke, is this your first carjacking?" Will asked as they walked along.

"It is," Luke said.

"You're doing an outstanding job," Will said. "Maybe you haven't been carjacked before, but at least you know what the rules are."

They reached the car, and Luke stopped short of the driver-side door and waited for instructions. Will put one hand on his shoulder and turned him around. He told Allison to check him for weapons.

"Remind me. What are the rules, again?" Luke asked.

"Number one is 'The guy with the gun is always right,'" Will said while Allison checked Luke for weapons. Self-conscious about running her hands all over a stranger's body, she did her best to project an aura that portrayed her to be both hardened and experienced at the task.

"Good rule," Luke said. "What's the next one?"

"Rule two is 'see rule number one,'" Will told him.

"He's got something in his front pocket," Allison declared.

"They're just the keys to the car," Luke said.

"Grab them," Will said.

Allison realized Will was speaking to her. "Wha—I'm not reaching into his pocket. They're, like, way down in there, Will. By, like, his... junk." She whispered the last part to him.

Will stared at her with widened eyes. "Maybe don't use our real names during a carjacking? Hm?"

"Well—we should have reviewed the carjacker rules before you decided to start jacking cars," Allison said, feeling foolish. Her father, if he were still alive, would have cracked her across the mouth for making such a dumb mistake. Heat crept up her neck and into her cheeks.

"I can get the keys," Luke offered.

"Grab them nice and slow," Will said.

Luke did as he was told. Will motioned for Allison to take them, and she plucked them from Luke's outstretched palm. Allison waited for Will to dismiss their victim.

"Where were you headed?" Will asked.

"To my aunt's house," Luke said.

"And where does Auntie live?"

Luke hesitated, and Will wiggled the revolver to remind him of the rules. "On Benson. A mile or so from here."

"A mile? And you couldn't wait until you got there to take a leak?"

Luke hesitated again, but it wasn't out of noncompliance—he seemed to want to choose his words carefully. "It was a long drive, and I had a lot of coffee and—"

"Which way did you come? Did you take Highway 57?"

Luke wrinkled his forehead in confusion. "No, I got off the interstate and then just turned off here. I think 57 is that way a few more miles."

"When is the last time anyone talked to Auntie?" Will asked.

"Before... everything. But they shut everything down. I couldn't get out of New York until now," Luke answered. "I'm sure she's fine. The landlines are still down out here, and she always hated the mobile phone my mom bought her."

Will chewed at the inside of his mouth—a habit Allison would later think of as his quick-thinking face—before glancing at Allison to make sure she was on board. She knew what Will was thinking about, because she was thinking it, too. She agreed with a nod. They had to do it.

"Get in the car," Will said.

"I'm new to carjacking, but I think you typically just take the car. If you take the driver, too, that's not really carjacking anymore, that's kidnapping," Luke said, slowly and evenly.

"Well, I guess we're first-time kidnappers now, too," Will said. He wiggled the gun and repeated his earlier order. "In the car."

"No," Luke said.

"No?" Will repeated, his tone clipped and angry. "You were doing so well, Luke, with following the rules. Maybe it would help to know that we're first-time kidnappers but not first-time murderers. Hmm?"

Allison, afraid that Will might forget why they were abducting Luke to begin with, intervened. "Stop it, Will."

Both men looked at her, and she went on. "No one wants to hurt you or your aunt. We just need food and water and a warm place for Kid to sleep," Allison said. "But we can't leave you here, either. You might call the cops on us. So the deal is... we get what we need, and then we leave you alone. I promise."

Will aimed the gun at Luke's head. "We all got choices, Luke. You need to make yours. You can get in the car, or you can stand here and get shot in the head over it."

Luke's eyes flicked to Kid and then back to Allison. She watched him work out his very limited options, and then he glanced back to Will again. Eventually, Luke exhaled a shaky breath and got in the car without another word.

6

A Biological Threat Has Been Detected

DOCTOR LUKE WRIGHT, DNP, CMSRN-RNFA

Saint Cassian Hospital of Brooklyn
Brooklyn, New York
January 20, 2019
10 days pre-WPE

"We're out of hallways. We shut down the cafeteria last week and filled that up. I don't know where else you'd like us to put patients. The roof? Maybe you can ask the nursing assistants to hold umbrellas over the ICU patients' heads." While he talked, Doctor Martin flipped through a patient chart on a tablet by jabbing at the screen with his finger.

"Everything is bottlenecking at—"

Doctor Martin held up his hand. "I have fifty more patients to see, so if you have a solution, *Professor* Wright, just do it," he said.

"So because I teach now, I don't know how to run an emergency room anymore?" Luke asked.

"I don't know," Doctor Martin said, punching at the tablet some more. He looked up. "Maybe you can write a paper about it later and tell me what I did wrong here."

Luke let the remark pass. "We can't turn patients away. That's a failure of—"

"You think you can fix the problem? Fine. Fix it, and maybe we will start accepting patients again. Until then, it is not happening." Doctor Martin ducked into the cafeteria, recently closed and newly converted to house flu cases.

Luke took a deep breath, cracked his knuckles, and reminded himself that the goal had been to get permission to make changes that he, as a lowly volunteer, wasn't able to make. His mission was accomplished. He took a second to tap out a quick text to his mother that he was fine, it was just a flu surge, and then he went to work to fix the congestion in triage.

January 25, 2019
5 days pre-WPE

"I can't believe you volunteered for this insane circus," Doctor Martin said. "But I'm glad you did."

They were sharing Martin's peanut butter and jelly sandwich on the roof, where Martin had previously suggested they stash patients. It was a sunny day, with no umbrellas or nursing assistants necessary.

"I forgot how much it sucks to get zero sleep, but the rest of it is like riding a bike," Luke said between bites of his donated sandwich. "And I can't believe I was happy to see a run-of-the-mill, old-fashioned knife wound this morning."

Martin chuckled. "Cowboy."

It was the strangest flu they had ever seen, with symptoms ranging from severe to mild, and completely undetectable on any test. Not that they had enough tests, anyway.

Luke had answered the call immediately when they began spreading the word that the flu had overwhelmed the hospitals. He had not been a professor for very long, and he felt called home and didn't hesitate to sign up. The university canceled classes until February because of the flu emergency, something they said hadn't happened since the early 1900s.

Martin wadded up the empty sandwich bag and dropped it in his pocket for disposal later. "Well, when I go back down, we'll start accepting wagons again. If we don't get buried up to our eyeballs in EMTs, then I'll fully open."

"What do you think this is?" Luke asked.

"I think it's mostly 'status dramaticus.'" Martin shrugged. "Aside from the occasional asthmatic that can't handle it, it's not too terrible. Just have to ride this storm out for another week, I think. The good news is that the nurses might give you shit here and there, but they like you. I overheard a couple of them talking at the desk."

"Good to know," Luke said. He texted his brother about their mother's upcoming birthday and sent him his half of the money for their gift.

Then they went back to work.

January 30, 2019
Day Zero

Luke hadn't slept in forty-eight hours, so he missed what the patient said the first time and had to ask her to repeat it.

"I said, he bit me. He just—he bit me."

"Who bit you?" Luke said. He examined her forearm with practiced care. The amount of blood made it hard to get an accurate assessment of the damage, and he would need to clean it up to get a better look at the wound, but he detected at least one distinct imprint of a tooth.

"My son. He just—he wasn't even a biter when he was a toddler!"

Luke examined the depth and circumference of the wound. "How old is he now?"

"Twenty-four."

Luke stared at her. "Uh—I'm sorry, your twenty-four-year-old son bit you?"

"Yes! He had that flu, so he was staying with me until he felt better. Anyway, I was ironing clothes when he bit me, so I smacked him with the iron and ran away."

"He didn't just bite you, he attacked you?"

"Yes, I—it was like he was someone—er, something else. And he was going to bite me again! I'm sure of it."

"I see," Luke said. He was going to have to file a report for the assault. But first they needed to get her cleaned up.

"When I ran away, I heard Mrs. Fogerty in 1A screaming. But I was so scared, I just ran all the way here. Something is going on. Something bad."

"We need to call the police anyway, so when we do, you can report the screaming you heard. Maybe they can do a wellness check on your neighbor," Luke said. "Right now, we need to get this taken care of, okay? I'll be back to get started on it, and then we'll have a doctor look. How does that sound?"

She nodded and wiped at her eyes with the floral sleeve of her other arm. Luke disposed of his gloves, grabbed the box of tissues off the counter, and handed her the box before leaving. He went to the nurse's station and picked up the phone, but he got a fast busy signal.

"Hey, are the phones down?" he asked one nurse.

She gave him a pointed look. "Does that work?"

Luke looked at the receiver in his hand. "No."

"Then the phones are down, Professor."

"Thank you for your help," Luke called to her back. He grabbed his cell phone and punched in 911, but the same busy signal sounded in his ear. There was an unread text from his mother, presumably received before the phones went down: was he coming home for her birthday? He made a mental note to answer her later when the phones were back up.

Luke went back to take care of his patient with the bite wound.

January 31, 2019
1 day post-WPE

"Does anyone know what happened to the flu? And why the hell do we have a waiting room full of bite victims? I'm kind of missing the flu right about now."

"What in the hell is going on out there?"

"How should I know? I haven't left this building in three weeks."

"What the—we're out of antibiotics? This is a hospital. We can't be out of antibiotics."

"Well, we are. On the plus side, we suddenly have plenty of beds."

"Hey, we got a wagon coming, three victims, all critical. One adult female, two children. Said the perp, uh—was eating them when the cops showed up."

"What in the actual fuck?"

"Well, there go the beds."

"What's that sound? Are those our phones? Are the phones working again? Why are they all going off?"

"It's a text."

"What's it say? I got my hands full here."

A hostile intruder(s) with unknown intentions may be on campus. Be aware of your surroundings, secure yourself behind locked doors, find other shelter or leave campus immediately. Follow instructions from emergency or other hospital personnel. Please limit phone use so phone lines are available for emergency messaging. Stand by for additional messages regarding this incident.

"Hey, Doctor Martin? Are you okay? You look kind of—"

"Oh my God."

"What the fuck is he—get him off her!"

"Security! Security! Somebody help me hold him!"

February 1, 2019
2 days post-WPE

WE INTERRUPT THIS PROGRAM TO ACTIVATE THE EMERGENCY ALERT SYSTEM.

This is not a test. Please listen to the following safety information. A biological threat has been detected. This is a national emergency. Take shelter in your home. Lock all windows and doors. Each family member must isolate themselves individually. Avoid contact with others. More information will be provided when it is available. Again, this is not a test.

THIS CONCLUDES THIS EMERGENCY ALERT SYSTEM MESSAGE.

Luke turned the waiting room television off after the message played for the third time.

"None of you has to stay here." Luke cleared his throat and went on. "I won't think any less of anyone that leaves. But I'm staying, and I'd sure appreciate any help that I can get."

There were a few shuffles of feet, and someone cleared their throat. Two people turned and left, and Luke watched them go before he went on. "That leaves one cardiovascular surgeon, a pediatric intern, one gynecologist, five nurses, and two nursing assistants. Everyone else is infected, dead, or went to be with their families. It's just us. That doesn't sound like much at all, I know, but for someone who makes it here, and needs our help, we're everything to them. So, I'm staying."

One of the nursing assistants spoke up. "I don't have anyone at home, anyway. Might as well stay here. I'm in."

"Me, too. Besides, I'm not going out there. I think we're safer in here until they figure stuff out."

There were murmurs of assent in the room before it quieted again. In the stillness, the steady thud of Infected beating useless fists against the doors of their hospital-rooms-turned-prisons filtered down to their ears.

"The cafeteria is stocked. We've got the entire second floor cleared for our personal use. Just pick a room and make yourself at home. I'll make out a rotation schedule, and we'll just do the best we can. When we aren't working, keep the door to your room closed. Until we know what is happening and how it's spreading, we have to self-isolate as much as possible in case—well, you know."

Luke, having worn the same scrubs for forty hours straight, went to the room he'd already picked for himself to grab a change of clothes and find a shower. Except there were no clean scrubs available, which meant going to the laundry and looking for some. He wasn't opposed to doing laundry; Luke had dated a girl who worked the midnight shift in housekeeping while he was in school at OSU. He used to help her get her work done quicker so she could take a much longer lunch break, and then he helped her with other things in his car in the one corner of the parking lot where the hospital security cameras couldn't reach.

Luke's dilemma was that the laundry was in the basement, and the combination of a subterranean location, poor lighting, and the incessant thumping of crazed cannibals in the upper levels of the hospital set the stage for a sinister undertaking. However, he'd just delivered an impressive speech, and his masculinity wouldn't let him ask anyone to go with him. Luke searched his room for something practical that he could take with him, but all he found was a flashlight, which he reasoned would be exceedingly useful in the event of a power outage. A blackout was extremely likely, according to every disaster film that Luke had ever seen in his lifetime.

Luke skipped the elevator, in anticipation of the prospective power outage, and took the stairs down to the basement. Once he reached the door that led from the stairwell to the basement, he pressed his ear to it and listened for several minutes. He and a few volunteers had already gone through each level of the hospital, but it seemed prudent to proceed with caution. Hearing nothing, he hesitantly opened it a few inches and peered out into the hallway. Seeing nothing, Luke opened the door fully and stepped inside.

He walked down the long hall to the laundry, mentally cataloging the various rooms he passed for future usefulness as he went. Once he reached the end of the corridor, he saw the problem. A giant cart under the chute overflowed with white cloth laundry bags. He was going to have to open, sort, and then wash—a process his former girlfriend must have accomplished before he'd shown up to help. For a moment he considered the ridiculousness of doing laundry in the middle of some sort of biological attack; but they needed to do their jobs, which meant having clean scrubs to put on. Luke wrinkled his nose in distaste at the chore before him, went to the storage closets, dressed in full PPE, and got to work.

While he quickly sifted through laundry, he let his mind wander. He worried about his family; the phones and internet were still out, and he had no information if what was happening in New York was happening all over or if they'd contained it to the city. His older brother would take care of his parents; he knew without a doubt that Mark would step up.

Luke's walkie went off. "Hey, we got a soldier up here. Says his unit lost their medic, and he's got a pretty nasty bite wound to his forearm." Luke recognized the voice. It was Diane, one of the nursing assistants.

"Okay, secure him in a room, give him the mask, and I'll be up in a minute," Luke said. One of the nurses was a coach for her sons' baseball team and had the team equipment in her SUV in the parking garage. The catcher's mask quickly became one of the most valuable items in their treatment arsenal.

The walkie chirped, and Luke thought he heard an echoing chirp coming from further down the hall, close to the laundry chute. He gathered up the items he'd sorted and swiftly got them into the washer and hoped the disinfectant would kill whatever the hell was responsible for a seemingly innocent flu that turned people into raging cannibals. Then he grabbed his flashlight and went to investigate the noise.

Luke reached the end of the hallway and paused. He tapped the button on his walkie and heard a twin sound coming from inside a door marked Housekeeping. He walked over and put his ear to the door and listened. When he heard nothing, he knocked and waited, but it was still quiet. Luke turned the knob slowly and pushed the door in just a few inches so he could peer inside. He saw shelving and no movement, so he opened the door a little more and found the walkie-talkie he was searching for.

The walkie was attached to a body slumped in a seated position on the ground—a man dressed in a security guard's uniform, with a badge that said "Luis" on it; he faced straight ahead, directly at Luke. His vacant eyes had a milky white pall over the irises. Glistening bone peeked out from beneath the chewed flesh of his right arm, and his bloodstained mouth opened and closed in a lazy, disinterested but steady fashion. The stench was unbelievable; Luke had been party to many unpleasant smells, but this mess had been closed up in a tiny room with no ventilation for who knew how long. He hadn't removed the PPE he'd put on to sort laundry, but he could smell it right through the mask.

Luke thought the man was dying, but he'd seen so many horror movies that he wasn't sure if normal biology ruled the people infected. The gun on the guard's hip tempted him; he thought it might be worth it to go over and find out exactly what basic principles of biology were still in effect.

Luke, with his flashlight still in hand, took a cautious step inside and was so focused on the security guard on the floor in front of him, he never heard the danger behind him until it was too late.

Saint Cassian Hospital of Brooklyn
Brooklyn, New York
February 1, 2019
2 days post-WPE

L uis Rodriguez had wanted to be a cop since he was a child, watching Miami Vice reruns on the television, and making his grandmother call him Tubbs before he would come to dinner. He maintained peak physical condition throughout high school by playing sports and hitting the gym daily, never missing, no matter what. Luis aspired to be a hero, and heroes didn't get days off from the gym just because they felt a little lazy that day.

Then his grandmother got sick, and frequent chemo appointments rained on his police-academy parade. He secured a position as a security guard so that he could pay the bills, and the idea was to apply for the academy later. Later turned to never, but Luis still played hero every chance he got, even after his grandmother passed away. Every Saturday from the hours of 1 p.m. to 3 p.m., Luis was the hero of the children's cancer ward by transforming himself into a popular comic book character. He even kept up his workout schedule; no beer bellies allowed for superheroes.

Luis had caught the weird flu that everyone was talking about, but recovered after a week and went back to work. A week later he felt a peculiar burning sensation in the back of his throat, and a ringing in his ears, just as he finished checking the basement during his rounds. He ducked into the housekeeping storage room so he could cough in isolation, concerned that he'd gotten the flu all over again. It worried him that he might let loose infectious germs into the air, but he was grateful that he was nowhere near the children's ward.

Luis coughed in the housekeeping room, and around the third cough, pain washed over his entire body. And just like that, he wasn't Luis anymore. But he was still a hero, because Luis, worried about nonexistent airborne spread, accidentally locked himself in the housekeeping storage room and kept the dwindling hospital staff from danger. He also provided Luke with a revolver.

Luke heard a growl just in time to spin around and raise his arms in a reflexive protective action; luck intervened in his favor and landed the long flashlight in his hand just close enough to the janitor's mouth for Luke to shove it between his teeth and keep the jaws from clamping down anywhere on his person. The janitor strained against the hard metal end of the flashlight, and it was all Luke could do to keep pushing back and not lose his balance. The janitor forced Luke into the storage room, and Luke's heel smacked against the leg of the security guard.

With threats looming on both sides, Luke's adrenaline kicked in, and he got a good push against the janitor, knocking him off-balance and backwards a few feet. The downside was that his mouth came off the flashlight, and the janitor lunged again, jaws open and hungry.

Luke swung the flashlight around and cracked the janitor as hard as he could, which was enough to stun the man into a momentary daze. Luke swung the flashlight again, this time sending the janitor sprawling backwards, his back hitting the doorframe whence they both came.

Luke checked to make sure the security guard was still on the floor. Luis turned his face upwards, clearly tracking and interested in Luke, but he hadn't risen. A growl came from the doorway: without time to worry about whether the guard would attack him, Luke freed the gun from Luis's holster and spun back around to face the janitor. Luke squeezed the trigger three times; the janitor had launched himself towards Luke and didn't stop coming until the second shot caught him right between the eyes.

Luke whirled back around to the security guard, who continued to lie there, but was now moving his half-eaten arm in

Luke's direction, trying to grab at him. Luke shot him in the head as well, and Luis, a selfless man and beloved hero of the children's cancer ward, died instantly.

Luke staggered backwards and out of the room, still clutching the gun and shaking all over. At first, all he heard was a loud ringing in his ears. The gun had been exceedingly loud in that tiny room, and the noise reverberated. After a few minutes, he realized his walkie was going off.

"That was definitely a gunshot! Where is Luke?"

"Yeah, I'm here. Everything is fine. I'll be up in a second."

Luke walked back into the room and grabbed the item that had started it all, the walkie-talkie. He backed out carefully and closed the door behind him. He grabbed a laundry marker from the sorting table and wrote on the door in very large letters: INFECTED—DO NOT OPEN.

Luke peeled off his PPE, disposed of it, and went back upstairs with his flashlight, his new gun, and walkie-talkie. Guilt racked his every step; he'd taken a life. He'd deemed his own life more important than someone else's and ended theirs. He wrestled with the idea that it was self-defense, but then what about the second time?

Nausea threatened him; a bead of sweat dripped down his forehead and landed directly in his eye. The stinging momentarily distracted him from feeling like he might throw up, and he rubbed at it until he could see again.

When he got to the waiting room, the staff on call were on one side of the room. Natalie, the nurse from the oncology department, held the catcher's mask out in front of her. Diane was bringing a walkie-talkie up to her mouth, presumably to call Luke again, when he shuffled into the room. Opposite them both was a young man dressed in fatigues and nursing his right arm in front of him, his eyes angry and defiant.

"Luke, are you okay?" Diane asked. She took a few steps back, which Luke couldn't fault given recent events. Co-workers, patients, strangers—they all had one thing in common: one second they looked just a little off and the next they were attacking and eating people.

"I just killed two people in the basement," Luke said. Still stunned by what had just happened, he struggled to absorb what was currently going down in the waiting room. Diane and Natalie asked questions, but he ignored them. "What's going on here?"

The soldier put his hands up. "Whoa, easy there, man."

His reaction confused Luke until he remembered he was still carrying the gun that he had taken from Luis, the security guard. "What's going on here?" Luke repeated.

"He won't put on the mask," Natalie said.

Luke, a stranger to carrying a gun but a fast learner about the power it provided, pointed the gun at him. "Put on the mask and get in the exam room."

"Sure thing, boss," the soldier said, hands up. Natalie handed him the mask; he accepted it, moving slowly and always keeping his hands in sight.

"You disinfected this, right?" he asked.

"You have an arm that looks like it went through a meat grinder, and you're worried that the Little League catcher's mask might have some cooties on it?" Luke asked.

"Good point, Doc," the soldier conceded.

"Glad you think so. For the record, yes, of course it's disinfected. Now get in that exam room and close the door behind you. I'll be in to look at your arm in a minute," Luke told him. He kept the gun trained on him until the soldier was behind the door of the exam room. The room had windows along the hall side, so Luke could see the man sitting on the gurney, looking glum but compliant.

Diane and Natalie had a hundred questions, which he waved off. "Stay out of the basement. Tell everyone else, too. I just—I need a minute."

Luke ducked into the public bathroom just outside the waiting room. He set his gun down on the small ledge at the sink and turned on the tap, filling his palms with cold water. He doused his face in cold water several times and then grabbed a wad of paper towels from the dispenser and dried himself.

"I can do this," Luke told himself in the mirror. He hadn't signed up to be a leader, but that didn't matter because somewhere along the way they had decided that he was one, so he had to keep it together. Until a few weeks ago, he led classrooms of nursing students. He had been nervous, but he'd faked confidence then, and he could do it again. His on-call shift was four more hours.

Then he could lock himself in his room and fall apart if he wanted to. Until then, even if he had to fake it the entire time, he had to keep it together.

Luke walked back out and headed directly to the exam room. He set the gun down on the counter by the sink and asked the soldier to lie back on the gurney so he could strap him in. To his surprise, he did exactly as Luke had asked.

"This—it's all a good idea. I can't bite you with a mask on, and I can't turn on you while you're working on my arm if I'm strapped in. Will you tell them I'm sorry about before?" he said. "Name's Mark."

"Luke," he said and strapped the man down. "My brother's name is Mark."

"Luke. Mark. Your parents religious?"

"Yep."

"Mine, too. I got a sister named Mary, and a brother named John. My mother hasn't missed Mass in thirty-five years."

"Let's see that arm."

Mark held out his arm for Luke to look over. It was bad, but Luke had seen worse, and he wouldn't bleed to death. He was missing a chunk that probably measured ten centimeters wide and four centimeters deep. "Pretty nasty."

"So was the Wormhead that bit me," Mark said.

Luke frowned. "Wormhead?"

"Yeah, you know. 'Cos of the prion."

"No, I don't know. What prion?"

Luke began assembling the things he needed to clean the wound up.

"The thing making everyone flip out. They found it. Said it's like that thing they had with the cows—uh..."

"Mad cow disease?"

"Yeah, yeah. Except they named it Wormwood. Wormwood—Wormhead. Get it?"

"They figured out what's causing this?" Luke asked.

"Well, they don't know exactly how people got infected. Just that the ones that are infected—they got prions in their brains. They said a bite or a scratch ain't going to pass it, though. If you believe that."

That was worrying news. Prions weren't bacteria or viruses; in fact, prions weren't even alive. There wasn't a chemical agent in existence that could eradicate them, and short of an incinerator as hot as the sun, they couldn't heat sterilize for prions either. Prions were basically proteins that folded themselves incorrectly, but why that happened was still a mystery.

The only bright spot was that a person had to come into direct contact with the infected brain matter to become infected with a prion. Luke thought briefly to the two men whose brains he'd just sprayed all over the housekeeping storage closet and was grateful he'd been wearing full PPE for laundry duty.

"Have they said what the incubation period is?"

"The what?"

"The length of time between when a person gets infected and they go full Cujo," Luke explained.

"Oh, right. The eggheads said that people got infected at all different times, maybe even years ago. The wormhead prions went dormant, but you remember that weird flu that just went around? That was the prions uh... acclimating and preparing their environment. Which I guess means our brains. Then people started going full Cujo at the end of January, and it's been like that ever since."

"That's impossible," Luke said. It meant that any of them could already be infected and could turn any time, whether they were recently exposed or not. He hoped Mark was wrong.

Mark shrugged. "What do I know? I just shoot where they point me."

Luke frowned. "Those are your orders? Kill on sight? What if they develop a cure?"

"Only cure right now is a bullet to the head. So what happened in the basement?"

Luke held up the small syringe. "I have something for the pain. Small pinch."

"It don't hurt that bad."

"It will once I get started on it."

"Right. Pinch away, Doc."

"Nurse," Luke corrected him. He injected the novocaine a few centimeters from the worst of the tear. "I'm a certified trauma surgical nurse, and I have a PhD and teach Nursing 101, or at least

I did before everything in the world went crazy, but I'm not an MD."

"You got a PhD? Is that hard?"

Luke chuckled. "A little, yeah."

"They why diss the title? You're a doctor, yeah?"

"Good point," Luke said. He tossed his gloves, pulled up a chair, and double-checked that his workspace was set up properly. "Give that a few minutes to work first," he explained to Mark.

"You didn't answer my question. What happened in the basement?"

"You should know that we're out of antibiotics. We ran out a few days ago, and obviously, supplies haven't shown up."

"Well, at least I won't bleed to death," Mark said. "I'll just get gangrene or some shit."

"Hopefully not," Luke said. "I'm going to clean this out with an extreme attention to detail."

"That's why I got that shot, huh?"

"Yeah. To be honest, you should get more, but we need to ration it."

Mark shifted his body around and centered himself; he gripped the rail with his good hand, ready for the pain. "Knock yourself out, Doc."

Luke worked as quickly as he could; but it was slow going, and he wasn't sure that he wasn't wasting his time. A human bite was rife with bacteria on a good day, and it wasn't a good day. He doubted the prions were being passed by saliva, but he was making that assumption based on knowledge he'd gained from school, and so far, nothing was going down like he'd read in a textbook.

When he finished, he patted Mark so he'd know it was over. The man's face was white from pain, and though he kept his jaw clenched tight, he had never made a sound.

Luke cleaned up quickly and then told Mark that they would move him to a room. "You'll take the mask off when you get there, and you can move around freely, just with the door closed."

Mark nodded that he understood. Luke undid the restraints and then headed towards the door.

"Doc?"

"Yeah?"

"I get that you're probably having a hard time with whatever went down in the basement. But you gotta throw that 'do no harm' thing out the window. If you want to survive this thing, whatever it is, you are going to have to look after numero uno."

Luke picked up the gun from the counter and weighed his words carefully. "If I had done that, thrown out the 'do no harm' thing, and was just looking after myself, you'd be sitting on the sidewalk right now."

"I hear them. Banging on the doors and shit. Why on earth would you keep them around?"

"I was thinking there might be a cure, and then..."

"A cure? Jesus, I hope not. If I get it, you cure me with a bullet, okay? A monster is a monster. They don't just go back to being a man with a nine-to-five."

Luke motioned to Mark's freshly packed wound. "Try to keep that still. We'll get you some oral pain medication, too."

Mark grimaced. "Yeah, no problem there. Hurts like a bitch."

Luke ran into Natalie, and together they moved Mark to his own room. Once they had that task accomplished, they went to the waiting room to talk.

"What happened in the basement?" she asked.

"Uh—I went down to do laundry."

When Luke didn't elaborate, she crossed her arms in front of her chest. "I've done laundry for twenty-five years, and I've never shot anything while I did it, and I had boys. You know what it's like to have young boys and laundry? One time I pulled an entire frog family from a front jeans pocket. I screamed bloody murder, but you know what I didn't do? I didn't shoot anything."

"There were two Infected down there. One was locked in a storage room, and the other jumped me from behind."

"Oh my God," Natalie said. She started pawing at him, looking him over. "Did they bite you?"

"No, and that's another thing. Our new patient brought in some news, and we should have a meeting and discuss it."

"Yeah, I'll get everyone together. Are you sure you're okay, though?"

"Honestly, I'm worried about my exposure. But we'll have the meeting and talk it over and go from there. Say thirty minutes? I never actually finished the laundry."

"You're going back down there?"

Luke held up his gun and gave her his best "fake it until you make it" smile.

"Yeah, why not? I'm the Dirty Harry of Housekeeping now."

February 4, 2019
5 days post-WPE

Luke had been careless with his gun. It only had one bullet left, and he'd gotten into the habit of thinking it was useless, or at least nearly so. Which was why he'd casually set it down too close to Mark when he'd examined the wound, and how Mark had gotten ahold of it so effortlessly.

Mark held the gun to his temple. "Doc, I wrote a letter to my wife. It's in my right pocket."

"Listen to me. You have a fever because your wound got infected. We knew that this might happen. You're not infected with the prion."

Natalie and Diane were in the hall, watching from behind the safety of glass.

"You don't know that, though, right? You never even heard of Wormwood before I got here, so I know you don't got no test kits lying around. You don't even have antibiotics."

"You're right," Luke said with his hands up. "We're out of antibiotics. That's why you have a fever." He took a step towards Mark.

"Leave the room, Doc. Don't want my brains getting on you."

"I'm not leaving. Because you will not shoot yourself. You don't need to. You've got an infection from your wound. That's it."

"So what, you're going to toss me a couple aspirin and call it a day, huh? Go get some golfing in?"

"I don't golf, but if that's what you want to do. Sure, we'll go golfing."

Mark gave a dry laugh. "I was a caddy at a country club one summer. The rich people's world is a whole different world. Man,

I bet they're still there trying to make par while we're out here sweating the whole goddamn thing."

"Well, we can go find out. Just put down the gun."

"Sorry, Doc. I've seen what they do. I won't turn into that."

Luke thought fast. "Your wife. What would your wife say if she was here? Think about her."

Mark sighed. "I am thinking about her." His mouth twisted into something grim. "She's already dead. Probably everyone is."

Mark squeezed the trigger, the wall beside him an instant painting of blood and brains. His body slumped over and lay still on the gurney. Luke stared at the wall beside Mark as the blood dripped down the wall, as the bits of brain matter and skull shards slipped off and fell to the floor.

His ears were ringing so loudly from the gunshot that he didn't hear Natalie or realize she'd come into the room until she grabbed his arm, making him jump.

Luke let her pull him from the room, but he stood at the window for hours and stared inside, until Diane eventually came by and made him go lie down in his room.

8

I'm From the Government and I'm Here To Help

Saint Cassian Hospital of Brooklyn | Brooklyn, New York
April 5, 2019
65 days post-WPE

After breakfast and a vigorous calisthenic workout session, Luke started the day with rounds. It was a new routine he was trying out, and so far, he found it to be quite agreeable. First, there was Mr. McCreary. Luke picked up the chart affixed to the outside of the door. "Mr. McCreary came in on February 1st presenting with a high fever and a cough." Luke listed off a rundown of tests performed to date. Luke loudly knocked on the door, prompting a faint growl from the other side. "Mr. McCreary has been listless the past few days. Most likely depression from the isolation he is experiencing. We're thinking perhaps a consult with psych."

Luke paused for questions, but there were none because, aside from the imprisoned Infected, he was completely alone and had been for three weeks now.

The next room had a narrow window that went from floor to ceiling. Luke grabbed the chart. "Timmy Parsons is a nine-year-old boy with advanced Wormwood Prion Disease." Timmy's face pressed against the glass, which was opaque with blood and saliva, his teeth scratching it as he tried to bite through the pane, hoping to chew his way out of the room and feast on Luke. An arm, ravaged to the bone by his incessant chewing, lay useless in his lap.

Luke crouched down and put his hand on the glass, obscuring Timmy's mouth. The child, excited by the possible contact with Luke's flesh, pressed himself harder against the window. He screeched with frustration when his efforts were in vain.

"I hope that with a cure, he'll make a full recovery. A prosthetic limb and a little physical therapy and... yes, full recovery."

Luke stood up. Rounds went until lunchtime. When he finished, he ducked into a bathroom and threw some cold water on his face. He stood there, watching drops of water run down his cheeks and chin. "Luke Wright. Patient needs a psych consult as soon as someone shows up to that department. Or any department."

He stared at himself in the mirror until it bored him, which didn't take long. His new beard was shaggy and unkempt; his skin was pale, and he had dark circles under his eyes from the lack of sleep. He was the only human being he'd seen for weeks. When Natalie had left, she'd begged him to come with her, because she didn't feel right about leaving him alone there.

"I need to know if my family is okay. You understand, right?"

Luke had understood. But he stayed, anyway.

After lunch—dry ramen noodles that crunched between his teeth followed by the last of the bottled water—he went down to the public waiting room and prepared to see new patients.

The barricade he'd erected wouldn't be effective against a regular person, but it wasn't meant to be. He'd constructed it so that any Infected would just shamble on by without gaining entrance to the hospital. Luke removed the barricade and carried out the large A-frame sign that he'd found in the gift shop. It now said "OPEN TODAY 1 PM - 5 PM." He erased yesterday's date and replaced it with the current one.

He thought, not for the first time, that he could just leave. He stood a few feet outside the hospital doors, wavering. Ultimately, as he had every other day, he went back inside.

He trudged into the waiting room, where he sat down and then... waited. He had been setting up shop daily, but it had been weeks since he'd last seen anyone. Luke passed the time by rearranging the magazines and disinfecting the public surfaces, and finally, some light dusting, but after three hours he still had no patients to see. Bored, he sat on one of the uncomfortable chairs and, listening to the dull buzz of the overhead florescent lights, dozed off. He dreamed that he was the last person left alive on the entire planet. It was an emotional dream; not a lot of imagery, but plenty of powerful feelings.

He startled awake, sometime later, to a room full of camouflage.

"Jesus, Mary, and Joseph!" a man exclaimed. "Kid, I thought you were dead."

The owner of the voice stood over him, grey-haired and confident, with an olive-green uniform that had some bars and things signifying him to be someone of importance.

"I'm not dead."

"I see that. What's your name?"

"Luke. Luke Wright."

"Are you here by yourself?"

"Yes," Luke said. "Well, it's just me and my patients. They're infected."

"Your patients?" the older man asked. "Do you have Biters here?"

"Do you mean Infected?" At the man's affirmative nod, Luke went on. "Yeah. In their rooms. Isolated, of course."

The man's brow wrinkled, and he pursed his lips. "Show me."

"Sure. One thing, though. Who are you?"

He motioned for Luke to get up. "Let's walk and talk, son. I have a schedule to keep."

Luke still felt disoriented from a combination of the nap, sudden wakefulness, and the room of gun-toting soldiers wearing hard plastic masks with respirators on them. He did as the man asked and led him to the stairwell. A handful of soldiers followed but stayed five paces back. When they left the waiting room, a bustle of activity began behind them. Luke looked back to see the remaining soldiers clearing out the waiting room.

"What are they doing? I just cleaned that—"

"I am Lieutenant Colonel George Carmel with the United States Army. We're commandeering this hospital for our use."

"Can you do that?" Luke asked, confused. "Just take the hospital, I mean."

"Congress has declared martial law. I can do whatever the fuck I want."

"They did?" Luke asked.

The lieutenant colonel stopped walking. "How long have you been here?"

Luke thought about it. "Since January. I volunteered because of the flu and then just—one thing led to another, and I never left."

"I see," the lieutenant colonel said. He took a step forward, so Luke resumed taking stairs again. "And how long have you been by yourself?"

"A couple weeks, I guess. Natalie was the last one, but she wanted to check on her kids and grandkids."

"You don't have anyone to check on?"

"I do, but they're all the way in Ohio. I have no survival skills, a gun without bullets, and these," Luke motioned to his hospital scrubs. "Didn't think I'd make it very far."

"You were right. New York was hard-hit, and you probably wouldn't have made it out of Brooklyn."

The lieutenant colonel's words made him worry about Natalie. He stopped ascending the stairs and turned to face the older man. "How bad is it?"

"Numbers are still coming in. It's pretty bad, but the human race is certainly not extinct. Not by a long shot. And now, they think they have a cure."

It took a second for the idea to sink in, but when it did, Luke's reaction was immediate. "A cure? Really? That's—That's great! Oh my God, that's fantastic."

The lieutenant colonel didn't seem to think so. "Hmm—well, our orders are to round them up and ship them in. Are we almost there?"

"Yes. Right. Sorry," Luke said. He turned back around and bounded up the stairs a few at a time. When he reached the third floor, he paused at the door and let the older man catch up before he opened it and stepped into the hallway where the very faint moaning and growling of the Infected filled the corridor.

"I was getting worried. You know?" Luke said. "I thought they were going to die waiting."

Lieutenant Colonel George Carmel walked briskly down the hallway, his polished shoes clipping along until he came to Timmy's room with the narrow window. "Are they all as advanced as this one?"

"Well, I don't go into the rooms. So I don't know, for sure, but, uh—he was one of the last patients to come in, so I guess the others are probably more advanced than he is."

He gave the soldiers behind Luke a signal; they filed out and assembled in the hallway.

"So... how are you moving them? Mostly, they turned in the room while they were alone so we just left them in there. But a couple I had to tie up and drag in," Luke said.

"Son. The cure only works on the ones that have been, well, not to put too fine a point on it, eating well. These here are all starved. When they don't have us to eat, they start chewing on themselves, like this poor little bastard here."

Two soldiers in front of Mr. McCreary's room made a few hand motions at each other and then one of them reached out, opened the door, and fired two shots into the room.

Luke tried to stop them. He tried to appeal to them. He explained they were just sick. He cursed at them. He apologized. He appealed some more.

They slaughtered them all. The hands that had held him back let go after they fired the last shots.

"Third floor is clear. Send in the torch crew."

"Roger that."

The soldiers left to check the remaining floors. The lieutenant colonel was the last to leave, and he clapped a hand on Luke's shoulder. "Go home. Not to Ohio. The borders are all closed. But I assume you live somewhere close by. Go there. You did the best you could, but the army will take it from here."

With that, the lieutenant colonel turned on his heel and marched to the stairwell and down the stairs. Luke was alone. He couldn't move at first. But then some morbid curiosity pulled his shuffling feet down the hall, past every single room that had been hidden to him by the closed, windowless doors.

The dead were grotesque. Gnawed-on limbs, poisoned by gangrene; putrid faces frozen eternally in agony and rage. Luke shambled past each room deliberately, taking in each one, filing them away for his future nightmares, of which he would have plenty. He lingered at Timmy's room the longest; stared at the baby teeth that had gnashed at Luke every morning when he went past. The teeth that would have loved to not have a pane of glass separating them. He moved on.

When he reached the end, the door to the stairwell opened, and a fresh crew of soldiers filed into the hallway, presumably the torch crew. Dressed in full PPE with hoods, they carried a large cart that was opened to reveal body bags.

Upon seeing him, the leader slipped off her plastic hood and approached him directly. Her brunette hair was pulled back into a ponytail; she had olive skin, and her brown eyes were sharp when she spoke through her hard plastic mask. "You're the guy, I take it."

"The guy?"

"The one that kept the hospital open."

"I guess I am. Nobody came, though. Just a couple after Mark and then no one since Natalie left."

She looked him over. "Do you have a place to go to?"

"I have an apartment," he said. "I just moved there a few months ago." He wasn't sure why he added that last part. The conversation, the woman, the hallway—none of it felt real. Maybe, he thought, he was still asleep down in the waiting room. That would explain everything.

"Where at?"

"They killed them all," he said. He felt dumb after he said it. She already knew that; she was the torch crew, whatever that was.

"Yes." She said it simply, without reservation. "Because they hadn't been feeding. The cure won't take, according to the eggheads. Do you know what that makes you?"

Luke was confused. "No."

"They're incurable because they weren't roaming around killing people. You saved a lot of lives by keeping these ones locked up. That makes you a hero."

"I'm not."

"You are in my book. Let's get you a transport and get you home. How does that sound?"

He didn't know how that sounded. The hospital was home. But they were taking it. He felt sick to his stomach suddenly, and it must have shown on his face because she stepped back just in time for him to throw up his dry-ramen-noodle lunch all over the floor in between them.

They ushered him back down to the waiting room, where a faceless soldier issued him a mask like theirs and gave him a jab in the arm. "It's a vaccine."

"Then why do I need the mask?" Luke asked.

"Because, just like the cure, they don't know if it actually works yet," was the answer.

From there, outside the hospital to a waiting Humvee. Parked twenty feet from the hospital, it was further than he'd ventured from the building in months. Halfway to the vehicle, he halted, suddenly afraid to go any farther. He was sweating buckets; he couldn't breathe, and his heart raced and thumped loudly in his ears. His hand ripped the mask from his face, and he gulped the air greedily, but still couldn't catch his breath.

There was an argument regarding getting him to move. One person posited they should just drag him, when someone came along and stopped the arguing. The woman with the olive skin and brown ponytail was next to him again. "Luke, is it?"

"Yeah."

"Okay, Luke. One more step."

Luke put a single foot forward. He gasped for air.

"Good job," she said. "You think you got one more in there?"

Luke did.

"I know it's hard. But that's all you have to do. Just one step. Then one more."

He nodded. "Can I just have a minute?"

"Sure." She stepped away from him and he heard her tell someone to just stand down a few minutes.

Luke closed his eyes; the sun had set, and the breeze was cool. He took a deep breath of the fresh air and exhaled slowly. It was real. They were real. The truck they wanted him to walk to was real. He was really going to his apartment.

But that meant they had also really killed them all. The Infected patients couldn't be cured or saved; in fact, he'd prolonged their suffering by keeping them locked up that way. He wasn't sure how he was supposed to just go back to his apartment and live there like nothing had happened.

She was back. His few minutes must be over. "One step."

He opened his eyes and nodded. He put on the mask they'd given him, and he walked away from the hospital, one step at a time, and climbed into the truck. As they pulled away, he watched the side mirror; the looming building shrunk little by little until it disappeared completely.

Luke never saw it in person again. He would go back in his dreams, though. The army would hold him down while the dead sprang back up in their rooms like deranged marionettes on strings and had their vengeance on him—they devoured him alive every night, starting with his heart.

9

Welcome to Citizen Freedom

Crowe Luxury Apartments | Brooklyn, New York
February 29, 2020
395 days post-WPE

"I 'm all packed," Luke said into the tablet. "Just have to hit the road."

"How do you feel about that?" his therapist asked. Six months ago, Congress hinted about resuming normal activities, and when the response from an agoraphobic republic was less than enthusiastic, they established a network of paid therapists to help ease the citizens back into a routine. Gloria Pulford was Luke's government-appointed therapist.

Luke held his draft papers up to the camera. "I feel great."

"C'mon, Luke, no deflecting. How do you feel about being drafted?"

"I feel angry that they can ignore my conscientious objector paperwork and call it a normal processing delay. I feel nervous about—well, everything involved with basic training. And I'm afraid that I'm going to shut down the second I have to hold a gun in my hand."

"That's better," Gloria said. "And that's a lot. Let start with the first thing."

They unpacked for a solid forty-five minutes. "Have you spoken to your father?"

"Aren't we out of time yet?"

"You have ten more minutes."

"Awesome."

"Luke?"

"No, I have not spoken to him yet."

"I think it's important that you keep trying to connect with him."

"I had to teach my last class this morning. I wasn't putting it off." He felt the need to defend himself. "I'm calling him next."

There was a brief pause. "Try to remember that we each have our own process to work through. I know you miss your brother and your mother. But your father has his own trauma, and he will have to forgive your brother in his own time."

They were easy words but hard done, as Luke's uncle used to say. Which brought him to the entire reason he wanted to squeeze a last session in before he reported for duty. "On my way, I'm checking on my aunt. The phones are back up in her area, but we can't reach her. The sheriff there said he's too overwhelmed with wellness checks to get to her before the weekend, so I'm doing it myself."

"Are you sure that's a good idea? Can't your father or another family member—"

"I'm the only one. Pop is on the West Coast with his sister, and I don't have any other family."

"I see."

"Any advice?"

"Yes, I don't think you should do it."

"I have to. I mean, someone has to."

"That someone doesn't have to be you. They're sweeping the towns to clear them and—"

"With slave labor. They're using the cured citizens as slave labor to clean up everything."

"Luke, this isn't—"

"I own the house now. My uncle died a few years ago, and they didn't have any kids. My aunt left everything to my brother and I. I just—I feel responsible for her and the place. It should be me."

Gloria nodded at him; the feed gave a warning blip.

"Hey, Gloria, I'm about to lose you."

She opened her mouth, and her lips moved, but there was no sound. "Shit," Luke said. He picked up the tablet and tried to move it to a better spot in his apartment, but eventually the screen went dark.

"Goodbye, Gloria."

Luke stood in the middle of his nearly empty apartment, surrounded by stark walls. Not quite warm enough to enjoy an open window, Luke had it open anyway—the comforting sounds of light traffic on the roads below filtered into the room along with the fresh air. He pulled out a prepacked lunch of peanut butter and jelly and sat down on the floor, cross-legged, chewing slowly and monitoring the modem, watchful for the green light to show that the internet was restored.

In the room's corner, a permanent indentation of the carpet marked the spot where Luke's television had stood. The open window was performing the function that the television used to have before he packed it and shipped it to his new address. The sound turned down, it had always been on—reassuring Luke day or night that the world was still out there, working.

A piece of mail sat on the floor in front of him. The outside of the envelope invited Luke to subscribe to a magazine entitled "Green Life." The torn flap, rough and turned up, made the neat rectangular envelope look like a tiny house with a roof on it.

Last September, a group calling themselves "Citizen Freedom" had infiltrated the Temporary Recovery Center in Nevada and produced a whistleblowing video series. The United States Army and Zakaria Pharmaceutical had been working together, but instead of curing and rehabilitating the Infected, like they were supposed to be doing, they were torturing and experimenting on them. The videos went viral, and Luke had a vested interest in watching the stomach-turning videos: his brother Mark was in some of them.

The modem turned green; Luke grabbed his phone, but the little white envelope in the corner showed no new messages. He set it back down.

It had taken a while to track down the group that posted the videos, and longer still to wait for a reply to the email he'd sent, where he unloaded his entire story. Luke left nothing out: his brother Mark and his death in the Relapse Riot outside Vegas; everything about the hospital, dwelling overly long, perhaps, on his perceived guilt and culpability in the suffering of others. Luke unburdened himself fully to nameless, faceless strangers and put himself at their mercy.

A response came three weeks later; he almost missed it, mistaking it for junk mail. The only reason he hadn't tossed it out unopened and unread was because the return of mail service was still novel, and even mundane spam held an appeal. The outer envelope invited him to subscribe to some automobile-mechanic magazine, but inside was a handwritten letter and instructions to join a private server. He was in. He was a proud member of Citizen Freedom, or as they called it, the CF.

`Welcome aboard.`

His membership involved light online duties; posting videos and keeping the signal boosted about the living conditions and legal rights for cured citizens. The rest of the time he hung out in the "lounge" area, where members could talk about anything. They saved his life.

He checked the phone again. Upon seeing the tiny "1" in the corner, he jabbed at it with his index finger.

`Good luck, brother. Remember, you are never alone.`

After the hospital and the extended period of continued isolation, Luke was embarrassed by how desperate he was for everyday human contact; to shake someone's hand or a simple pat on the shoulder. It bothered him so much that, before his admittance into the CF, he'd thought more than once about maybe taking more of his prescribed "nightmare" pills than he was supposed to, and letting the cards fall where they may.

The CF didn't cure his craving for simple human contact, but they gave him hope. It was a family, a brotherhood, and sisterhood—it connected him to people who felt the same way he did.

His sandwich finished, Luke picked up the junk mail that sat on the floor in front of him. He pulled the paper out and read it for the hundredth time.

`Don't dodge.`

Initially bewildered by what it meant, two days later he'd received his draft notice.

Luke called his father. Pop was uncomfortable with technology, so it took several attempts of Luke calling, getting hung up on, and then Pop calling Luke back before they finally connected.

"Hey, Pop. Can you see me?"

And they were off. They talked nonstop for thirty minutes about almost nothing at all, the ghost of Mark sitting in on the entire conversation. Luke did his best. He didn't want to upset his father by bringing Mark up, but sometimes the subject burned in his throat and if he didn't say something, he thought he might burn alive.

"They want to do a memorial wall outside of Vegas. I filled out the paperwork to get Mark's name added—"

"Don't you ever say that name to me."

"C'mon, Pop. It wasn't his fault. He was sick—"

"I have to go."

"Wait—I'm sorry!" Luke didn't know when he'd be able to talk to his father again. "I'm sorry. Let's, um, let's talk about something else. I leave today so I can report by next Friday."

His father didn't answer; he looked at something offscreen, deciding whether to accept Luke's terms to just change the subject and talk about something else, or end the call. He wouldn't allow Luke to love his mother and his brother at the same time. It was another reason Luke loved the CF; they let him love and miss them both without guilt.

"I didn't think I'd see them restart the draft in my lifetime."

"Nobody did, Pop," Luke said, relieved they were still talking. "At least, not like this."

"I still don't see how it's legal to pull civilians into active combat situations without a lick of military training," his dad went on. Luke had chosen an excellent subject to get his father going on; he quickly forgot all thoughts of Mark as he ranted about freedoms being trampled and liberties being extinguished.

"They need nurses," Luke said when he could get a word in. "And I'm going to basic training, but the combat part is pretty much over now."

His father made a disgruntled noise.

"I'm swinging by Aunt Cece's on my way to Cincinnati to check in."

"You—I don't think you should go."

"You and my therapist both," Luke noted, dryly.

"Well, I don't like that head-shrinking stuff, but this time I agree with her. I just—you had a bad time, son. It's not a good idea to jump right into another unpleasant situation."

"You know, everyone keeps assuming Aunt Cece isn't okay. She's probably there, making pies and feeding them to Georgie. Poor dog is probably diabetic by now."

His father didn't laugh at his joke. "There are companies now, they offer services. They'll go in and clean up the house and get it ready for sale."

"There isn't a reason to sell the house if Aunt Cece is just making pies."

"Luke—you can't honestly think that—"

"Dad? Dad?" Luke pretended not to hear him. "You're breaking up. I think I'm losing the feed."

"Infernal contraptions! Can you hear me?"

"Dad?"

Luke ended the call and turned the tablet facedown. While he pulled on his lucky hoodie, he wondered what his mother would think of him. That thought was a bit like accidentally grabbing a pan with a hot handle, so he dropped it. He switched gears: Aunt Cece was his mother's sister. They were two years apart in age, but they looked so much alike they could almost be twins. He was really looking forward to seeing Aunt Cece again.

In the new-to-him Accord, Luke's road trip materials lay on the passenger seat: cash for the turnpikes, his vaccine booster card, passport, and military-provided gas ration cards, and last, draft papers to satisfy his permissible travel purpose. The car was otherwise empty; most of Luke's things already shipped via freight so he could insure them. Highway pirating had become a fast-growing enterprise, and the forecast for his route was poor.

Luke drove off into the early afternoon sun to a small town called Harmon's Folly; hoping for a mundane journey and a total lack of adventure.

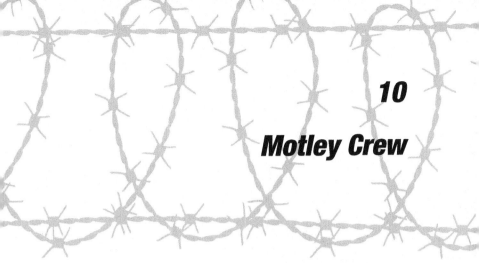

10

Motley Crew

Harmon's Folly, Pennsylvania
February 29, 2020
395 days post-WPE

L uke's captors were a motley crew—with hackneyed haircuts, visible bruises and needle holes peeking out from collars and sleeves, they were underweight with pale skin and dark circles under their eyes. The Citizen Freedom family had declared the final shutdown of all Temporary Recovery Centers to be a victory last night, and Luke was fairly certain their victory was currently holding him at gunpoint.

"I'm Allison," she said. Allison had Will's gun and was sitting in the passenger seat. When he didn't acknowledge her introduction, she bit her lip and set the gun down in her lap. With the gun no longer pointed at him, Luke relaxed a little and offered a polite reply that it was nice to meet her.

The man in the back kicked under her seat. "And that grump in the back is Will. And that sweet little girl back there is Kid."

"Her name is Kid?" Luke asked.

"It's as good a name as any." Allison shrugged.

Luke kept her in his peripheral vision. She seemed more interested in the landscape they were passing than watching him, her hostage. She was drinking it all in, a tourist in a mundane destination, somehow finding it all to be thrilling.

"Is she your daughter?" Luke asked. He turned his attention away from the road for a moment. Allison had fixed her attention completely on him, all other vistas and sights cast aside for Luke. Something about her expression combined with the gun on her lap unnerved him. His hair stood up on the back of his neck, and he held his breath. In various biology classes he'd dissected different animals, all the parts spread out on wax slabs with push pins. That was how he felt just then: pinned down, taken apart, and examined.

"She is now." After she spoke, she went back to looking out her window—the pin she'd placed in him lifted, and he could breathe again. It occurred to him that he'd just taken a dangerous test and had somehow passed.

His mouth was dry. He remembered the road and whipped his head back to it. He cleared his throat. The next question was out before he could stop it. "Is he your father?"

The corners of her mouth quirked up a little, but she didn't answer. Luke looked in the rearview mirror again. Will was not the slightest bit amused by the question.

"Right," Luke said, realizing. He resisted the urge to look in the rearview again—Will was easily fifteen years older than Allison. It wasn't Luke's business, but he felt outraged on her behalf. Luke felt Will's eyes boring a hole in the back of his head. He needed to steer the conversation away from this topic and fast.

"Where are you headed?"

Will interrupted. "Don't worry about where we're headed," he barked. "Worry about driving this car to your aunt's house. Got a kid back here that needs some food and water. And turn the heat on, we're freezin'."

Will interrupting their conversation and bringing up the little girl threw cold water over Allison's conversation skills. She laid one hand over the gun in her lap and fell silent the rest of the way to his Aunt Cece's.

His aunt lived in a big farmhouse, on land that she used to farm until her husband died. They had no children of their own, but Luke and Mark had spent many summers there, playing in the woods behind the farm, chasing chickens, or helping Uncle Rodney with chores. She'd refused to sell the house and said she'd live there until the day she died.

He pulled into the driveway; it was dirt and gravel and nearly a quarter of a mile long to get to the house. Luke resisted the urge to spring out of the car and run in to warn her to get away. Instead, he waited for one of them to give orders again. They seemed to be reasonable, as long as he was compliant.

"How do you want to do this?" Will asked him.

His heart raced. "What do you mean?"

Allison and Will shared a look.

Will answered him. "Your aunt might be fine, yeah. But if she's not okay, and she's still, uh, bumping around in there... she can't be cured. It would be too late. You know that, right?"

Luke knew that very well. He looked at the gun that was on Allison's lap, under her other hand. "No, she's probably fine."

"If she's been in there alone this entire time, starvin', it would be a kindness. I promise you that."

For a moment he was back in the hospital, standing alone in a hallway with open doors. He took a deep breath. "No. I—um—I'll go knock, and if she doesn't answer, then—"

"You seem like a nice kid," Will said. "Why don't you just stay here and let us sort out things in there, huh?"

Something about Will calling him a kid and using a soothing, condescending tone pushed a button in Luke. "You think I can't handle it? That I somehow survived because I was what? Lucky? You think I didn't have to fight to survive?"

"Fight?" Will asked. "You want to go in there and fight your dear auntie, you go right ahead. But what she needs is killed."

"You think I haven't had to kill anyone?" Luke asked.

Will didn't answer him, but Allison did. "That person you had to kill. Did you love them?"

It was a simple question—but for the second time that day, she took his breath away. When he didn't answer, she held the gun out to him. "Here. Take it, then."

"Al—"

Luke took the gun from her hand before Will could intervene. He was so stunned by his changed fortune that he forgot to point it at anyone and instead looked at her for some explanation.

"That gun doesn't matter too much if there ain't no teeth behind it. Do you have the teeth to put behind it?" she asked him. "Because unless you loved whomever you killed to get here, then what you gotta do right now for your aunt isn't even close to being the same thing."

Luke had stopped spending summers at his aunt's farm once he graduated high school. That said, he'd spent eighteen perfect summers there. Eighteen summers of his Aunt Cece spoiling him with attention, baked goods, and hugs. She loved them, and if she was alive, she'd side with Luke against his father about Mark. Things would be different, because Aunt Cece would make his dad listen, and Luke wouldn't have to choose—he could mourn his mother and his brother at the same time.

Luke had killed a security guard named Luis and a janitor whose name he never learned. He'd let an entire floor of patients live in prolonged agony because he'd clung too hard to the idea of a cure that wasn't possible for them.

Luke handed the gun back to Allison.

"AL." Will voiced his profound displeasure with Allison's generous policy regarding deadly firearms and hostages. Allison rolled her eyes and handed the gun over the seat back to Will.

Luke looked directly at Allison. "I'm going, too."

"Nope," Will declared from the back, checking the clip and then reinserting it.

"She's *my* aunt." Luke continued to appeal to Allison only.

"Will," she said. She wasn't looking at Will, though, she was looking at Luke.

"Oh, for the love of—" Will complained. "Fine. Kid and I will hang out and play thumb wars."

Will passed the gun to Allison once more, but didn't let go. The two stared each other down, but it wasn't until Allison grated out a tiny "Fine" that Will let the weapon go. Luke got out of the car and wondered exactly which one of them was in charge of their enterprise.

They headed to the back of the house; the front door was historically kept locked while the back door was left open. Allison stood next to the door, expecting to be let in like she was his guest. He was about to reach forward and open the door for her when something furry and wet jumped on Luke's back. Allison, alarmed by Luke's sudden movement, pointed her gun at the source of Luke's fear.

"Oh my God, Georgie?" He put his hand out for Allison to put the gun away and dropped to his knees in front of his aunt's border collie. "I can't believe it."

Georgie covered Luke's face in wet kisses immediately, while Allison's legs were beaten to a pulp by the dog's boisterous wagging tail. Luke attempted to examine Georgie, but it was impossible because the eager canine fought Luke off in favor of kissing his face and neck and hands.

"C'mon, Georgie," Luke protested. "Sit."

Georgie held renown for playing catch, playing chase, playing tag, and playing Frisbee. He was not well known for playing sit.

"I mean, he looks pretty healthy. So maybe..." Luke looked at the door hopefully.

Allison adopted that look again, as though she knew something that he didn't and felt sorry for him about it. He grabbed a tennis ball off the corner of the stoop that led to the back door and threw it as far away from the house as he could. When Georgie ran for it, Luke said nothing to her; he just put his hand on the door, flung it open, and stepped inside without hesitation.

Allison stepped in after him. Luke pulled the door shut behind her to keep Georgie from coming into the house after them. They stood inches apart from each other and held still, listening.

A floorboard creaked above their heads. Allison moved fast and stepped in front of him; she used her free arm to hold him back, her head tilted sideways and listening, barely breathing. She looked predatory, a surreal hunter in search of prey. Luke wondered to himself: Is this how Aunt Cece looks, right now, somewhere in the house? Is she hunting us?

The floorboard creaked again, and Allison pointed to the ceiling.

Without making a sound, she hurried over to the entranceway that led to both the living room and the stairs to the second floor. She peered up them, and after a few seconds of listening, she whispered to him. "Call her."

"What?" Luke whispered.

"If she comes down, I'll be able to see her face from here, and I'll know if she's fine."

"And if she doesn't come down?"

She made a face. "Then I'll have to go up."

11

Safety's Off

Harmon's Folly, Pennsylvania
February 29, 2020

"A unt Cece? It's Luke!"
The floorboard creaked, and then creaked again, but no one came down the stairs. There the shuffle of feet coming from above them, towards the front of the house. Then, a pounding, fists on a door.

Allison frowned; Luke's aunt was awfully ambulatory for a starved Biter. She was about to express this thought to Luke when he ran past her and bounded up the stairs two at a time. Allison gave chase and caught him standing in the hallway outside of a closed door.

The door banged rhythmically on its hinges. Allison sometimes struggled with text, but the words written on the bedroom door were scrawled nice and far apart so she could read it easily enough.

Don't open. Tke care Georgie. Love u. Feb 1, 2020

"I'm so sorry, Luke," Allison said. "It's too—"

Luke blinked back tears and nodded. "Is she in a lot of pain?"

His hands were balled up into fists, and he shoved them into his pockets, his shoulders hunched over so far that he suddenly seemed to be nearly her height. He'd shrunk before her very eyes. She considered sparing his feelings and lying to him.

"The truth," he told her.

"Are you sure?" she asked.

"I'm sure." He stared at the bedroom door.

"Yes. She's in a lot of pain."

"How bad?"

Allison took a deep breath. "Why do you want to know that? That's not going to help anyone."

"I just do. Will you tell me?"

Allison sighed. He was clearly bent on self-torture. "So crazy bad that... to make it stop... she'd chew through every single piece of you without pausing even once."

"Oh. That bad."

"I'll just—"

Luke put his hand out. "She's my aunt. I'll do it."

Allison paused, silently wished for Will not to find out, and then handed over her gun to Luke for the second time that day. "Do you know how to use it?"

"Yes," Luke said. His voice was small and distant. "Mostly."

"It ain't that hard. The safety's off so you just gotta point and pull the trigger."

"Sounds easy." He was visibly sweating, the knuckles of his left fist hard and white.

"We heard her walking around, so she's still on her feet." Allison put her ear to the pounding door, and then bent her knees, crouched down a foot before she stopped and put her finger on the spot to show him. "Right here, I think. Just shoot right through the door, and then I can go in and make sure."

"Through the door?"

"Well, she's against the door. If you try to force the door open, you'll probably end up getting bit. Won't infect you, but I imagine it hurts like a bitch."

Luke nodded, squeezed his eyes shut, took a deep breath, and then opened his eyes again. He didn't shoot. He was sweating more profusely, his face pale, and when he opened his eyes again, they were wide and afraid.

Allison put a hand on his outstretched arm. "Why don't you just let me do it?"

"I have to," he said.

"Who said so?" Allison asked. The question startled him. She didn't care; she put her hands on her hips and waited for an answer.

"No one said so, but—"

"Then why in the hell are you torturing yourself over this? Just let me do it. Why do you think we kidnapped you in the first place?"

"You kidnapped me because—"

"Because you seemed nice, and we didn't want to see you get yourself killed," Allison said. "So just give me the damn gun, Luke. And cover your ears."

He rubbed the back of his neck like it hurt, scowled briefly, but eventually gave her back the gun. She quickly fired into the door, before he could change his mind again, while he flinched hard with every shot.

People who hadn't been around guns before tended to be skittish; however, in Allison's opinion, Luke seemed to suffer from something a little more than gun virginity. It was quiet on the other side of the door, and she patted his arm to get his attention. He lowered his hands from his ears, and they trembled at his sides.

"I'll go in and check, yeah?"

Allison tried to open the bedroom door. There was a weight against it, so she threw her shoulder into it, forcing it open enough to duck her head inside. Satisfied that it was safe, she shoved her body against it again. Once she got it open a half a foot, she slipped inside and closed the door behind her.

The woman on the floor was a mangled mess, and the smell was absolutely unbearable. There were two windows in the room, and Allison opened them both. Allison had missed her head with the gun, so the woman's head was tracking Allison's movements. Her jaws opened and closed in hopeful anticipation of something to chew on.

"Dammit."

She knocked on the door twice and called out to Luke. "Hey, cover your ears again."

"Why?"

"Because... I missed."

"Oh my God."

"I'm sorry. Just—just do it."

Allison covered her nose with her shirt, which did absolutely nothing to dampen the putrid smell in the room. Allison shot her once more, and poor Aunt Cece fell over dead.

Allison grabbed a quilt off the bed. It was pretty, with complicated-looking calico stars on it—she hoped it wasn't some sort of family heirloom. She laid it down, and while she held her breath, she quickly dragged the woman over and wrapped her up like a mummy.

Luke was sitting on the stairs, halfway down, staring into space.

"Luke?"

He didn't answer.

"Luke?"

When he didn't answer her again, mindful of her dirty and germy hands, she tapped him with her foot. He startled back to the present.

"Sorry. Just, um—I covered her up so you can remember her however you want to."

"Right. Thanks."

"I'll give you some privacy and go get cleaned up. But stay in the hall, you shouldn't go in there."

He nodded, but he wasn't looking at her; he was staring past her into space again. She ducked into the bathroom at the top of the stairs and washed herself thoroughly, to make sure she wasn't carrying anything that could infect Luke.

"She looks exactly like my mom," he said when she came out of the bathroom. "Everyone said they could be twins."

"Yeah?" Allison asked.

"My mom's dead. My brother killed her, and my father will never forgive him. He's dead, too, my brother, I mean, but you know—I can't even talk about him to the one person who really remembers him like I do. And I just—If Aunt Cece's gone, then my mom is gone—she's all the way gone because there isn't anything of her here that's left now."

"Oh," Allison said, understanding. She sat down on the step next to him.

"You're here, though."

He looked at her, confused.

"She's not gone as long as you're still here, right?"

He ran a hand through his hair and then down his face. "I guess."

He looked up and wrinkled his brow. "Are you still stealing my car?"

"Uh—yeah. Probably."

He buried his face in his hands, and his shoulders shook. Allison thought he was crying, and she almost told him they'd just walk instead of stealing his car, but when he lifted his head, she saw he was laughing.

"Are you okay?" she asked him.

"No," he said, wiping his eyes. "I will be, though. Eventually."

"In the old days, I'd offer you a hug," Allison said. It wasn't entirely true since she was unlikely to offer hugs to strangers, but she was pretty sure Luke was on the verge of a breakdown of some kind.

He sobered a little. "But not now?"

"Well, no. Normals don't, um—" She wasn't sure how to politely explain, or why she needed to. "We kind of freak you people out."

He wiped at his eyes again. "You people. What is that supposed to mean?"

"Oh, I—uh..."

He laughed again. "Sorry—I'm sorry. I couldn't help it."

"I am definitely stealing your car."

He laughed harder. "Joke's on you because it needs gas."

"Seriously? Dammit, I don't have any ration cards."

"I'll sell you one."

"Sell me one? I have a gun, remember?"

"Yes, sell you one. One ration card for one of those hugs you spoke of earlier."

"You are that hard up for a date?"

"You have no idea." His cheeks turned pink, and he waved his hand. "I was joking, you don't have to—"

Allison set the gun down on the floor next to her and, before she could think too much about it, hugged Luke. He tensed immediately. Allison, thinking she'd read the situation all wrong, pulled back, but before she could get away, he reached out and hugged her back. Hard. Possessive. Long. His fingers bunched up her shirt. He smelled good; she thought of long summer days, backyards, and catching fireflies.

They were still hugging each other when Will came in the back door with Kid and the dog, Georgie. She could hear him calling for her, asking what was taking so long. He stood at the bottom of the steps, and upon seeing them clinging to each other for dear life, he yelled up the stairs at her.

"God dammit, Al. You are the absolute worst kidnapper in the world."

12

Point Zero-Zero-One

Harmon's Folly, Pennsylvania
February 29, 2020

W ill had broken whatever spell they had been under; they laughed at him while they disentangled themselves from each other, but it was suddenly awkward. They mumbled some small talk about finding something to eat and the need to bury his poor Aunt Cece, and headed downstairs together.

Will was poking around the kitchen. "First thing we should do is flush the pipes. Just go around and turn all the taps on and let them run for a bit."

She and Luke did as he asked; aside from the kitchen and upstairs bath, there was only a small commode and shower in the basement. It was a weird setup as they weren't behind any walls but in a corner of the basement—completely in view of the entire basement.

"I have no idea," Luke said as soon as he saw her looking at the random, unenclosed toilet. He turned the shower on to let it run. "And I definitely don't know why my uncle wouldn't have remodeled and built some walls."

The water came out rust-colored and then turned to a jet black; Allison wrinkled her nose at the smell. Luke asked her what was wrong.

"You don't smell that?"

"Smell what?"

"Nothing," Allison said.

Luke bent down closer to the running water and sniffed, experimentally. "I don't smell anything. What does it smell like to you?"

"Just bad."

"Like a chemical? Rotten eggs?"

"No, it's not like that. It's just—bad. I can't explain it. It's like a warning or something."

"A warning?"

Allison considered it for a second. "All smells warn you, I guess. If you smell gas, you know something's wrong. But anyway, if my eyes were closed, I'd know that water wasn't safe to drink by the smell of it."

Luke got excited; his eyes grew enormous, and he ran a hand through his hair as if he'd just won a lottery. "You have enhanced hyperosmia."

"I have what now?"

"Enhanced hyperosmia. An extremely sensitive and advanced sense of smell."

"Oh. We call 'em Sniffers at the Center. I made a lot of money off it for Will."

"You made money? In the Center?"

"Well, not cash. Whatever the currency was. On Monday it was pudding cups but on Tuesday it was cherry gelatin. Will says all money is made up anyway, and in the right settin' there's no difference between cash and gelatin cups. Anyway, Will had a betting pool he had started before I met him. When they'd bring in the gurney guppies—"

"The what?"

"Uh, the new fish. Guppies. They're still strapped down to the gurneys when they bring them in."

"Right."

"So anyway, we would all bet on which ones would wake up and which ones wouldn't. One day I figured out that I could tell just by walking by and sniffing. Will made so much that the Biters quit playin'. I told him he should lose once in a while, but he was just having too much fun, I guess."

After glancing at Luke's face, she felt a little embarrassed about the morbid speculation she'd engaged in. "Yeah, I guess it's kind of awful to bet on who lives and who dies."

"I'm not going to judge you," Luke said. "So how were you able to tell which ones would wake up?"

Allison shrugged. "Sometimes a smell makes me feel something. The rusty water made me feel sick. Or sometimes I'll see or think about something that seems completely random but has to do with the smell. Kind of like when you smell smoke, you immediately think of fire. I don't know, it's like a warning. So when I was sniffin' the guppies—I knew."

"Wow. That's amazing. And super rare. I think they said it was .001 percent of all the cured."

"They said at the Center that our noses led us around the entire time we were infected. Took us straight to uninfected people so we could—well, anyway, I guess the cure didn't one-hundred-percent take with me."

"That's not it. You're cured."

Allison remembered the soldier she'd killed the day before. "I'm not so sure about that."

Luke's eyebrows drew together, and he took a step towards her. "Why would you think that?"

She didn't tell him why, because she couldn't bring herself to give him a reason to treat her like the rest of the uninfected did—even though she was sure it was what she deserved. An image of her bloody hands flashed in her mind, and she changed the subject.

"The water smells good now. You can shut it off."

Luke turned the water off. "Listen, you probably have—"

Allison cut him off. "That number. The point-zero-zero-one or whatever. Do you know why it's so low? Because they pulled the other Sniffers into the back for their so-called follow-up testing, and those Biters never came back again. I'm alive because Will told me to shut up about it, and I listened."

He blanched. "I'm sorry. I was just—"

"I'm not trying to make you feel bad. I'm really not. But I don't want to be some fascinatin' specimen ever again. Not a single goddamn thing about me is amazing or interesting. Okay?"

He apologized again.

"Luke. Please stop apologizing. You're so damn polite that it's pissing me off."

"I'm sorry—oh my God."

Allison's face was on fire; she chided herself for losing her temper. "Forget it. We should go back upstairs. I need to find something to feed Kid."

Luke's aunt had a wide variety of food in boxes, jars, and cans. Allison chose the things that she assumed would cook up the quickest. Will helped by picking up the items, at random, and announcing the cooking instructions in such a way as to seem like he was making conversation rather than reading them aloud to her.

They ate quickly. All three Biters were starving, but Luke picked at his dinner and shared it with Georgie. Luke annoyed Will. Allison could tell by the way he watched Luke in his peripheral vision. She thought of this habit of his as "filing" because Will was creating a running list of everything that he perceived to be a weakness in Luke and "filing" it away for later use. She'd seen Will do it many times at the Center, and it was never good news for the person being filed.

Will sat at the head of the table; he sipped whiskey from a bottle that sat in front of him. The gun lay on the table within his reach. Allison scrubbed at the pots and pans in the sink while Kid took tiny nibbles of a chocolate cupcake. The box containing the rest of the cakes sat in the middle of the table.

"After supper we're going to handle your aunt," Will informed Luke over a bite of instant mashed potatoes. Allison took a deep breath; Will had finished filing. She quit the washing up and leaned back against the sink, ready to intervene.

"What do you mean, 'handle'?" Luke asked.

"Burial," Will said, and took another sip from his glass. He poured a second glass and then slid it across the dinner table to Luke, who caught it, spilling some on his hand.

"You don't have to—" Luke began.

"I wouldn't want you to become tainted. Besides, she's a Biter now, and we take care of our own," Will said.

Luke made a face.

"I'm sorry, I forgot Biter was politically incorrect. How about Previously Infected? Or Newly Cured?" Will asked. "Those work better for you?"

Kid finished the last of her cupcake, hopped off the chair, and made a beeline for Allison at the sink. She wrapped her arms around Allison's legs and watched Luke from a safe distance.

"Will."

When Allison said his name, Will leaned back in his chair, and made a big show of putting his arms behind his head, the picture of casual relaxation and small talk.

"Where to next?" Will asked.

"What?"

"You came here from New York? You going back there or staying here?"

"Neither," Luke said. He drained the glass of its contents and then set it down with more force than was required. "I have to report to Cincinnati by Friday."

Will's brow furrowed. "Report?"

"I got drafted," Luke explained.

Allison stood next to Will, Kid in tow. "What do you mean, drafted?" she asked.

"You know, selective service," Luke said.

Will did a double take. "How old are you?"

"Twenty-eight."

"They're drafting twenty-eight-year-olds?" Will asked.

"They're drafting forty-year-olds if they have a medical background. It's been all over the news for weeks," Luke asked. "How do you not—"

Will pursed his lips. "They didn't exactly provide us with television privileges in the RC."

"Right, sorry," Luke said. "Well, I applied for classification as a CO."

"What's that?" Allison asked.

"It means he's a conscientious objector," Will said. He looked up at Allison. "He's opposed to war and killing and stuff."

"I'm extremely opposed to unarmed American citizens with a curable illness being fired on by other Americans," Luke clarified. "But yes, killing in general is off the table. That doesn't matter, though, because by the time they process my claim I'll have already gone through basic."

"I suspect it also means that he's some sort of smarty-pants and they will get him to work for government wages instead of whatever he's actually worth." Will looked up at Allison. "Because he can do stuff that regular folks like me and you can't do."

Allison waited for Luke to confirm or deny Will's explanation. He hesitated; he seemed to be debating something with himself.

"I'm a nurse," he said.

"They don't have nurses in the army already?" Allison asked.

"Yes, but... a lot of people died," Luke said. "They're still counting, but almost two billion people died. And a lot of the Infected went to doctors and hospitals when they felt sick."

Allison put a hand on Will's shoulder and squeezed. "Hits a little different when there's a number on it."

Will put his hand over hers and gave Luke a pointed look. "We could probably do with a little less current events."

Kid began tugging at Allison's shirt, and Allison picked her up and balanced her on one hip while Will glowered at Luke over another glass of whiskey.

Allison kissed the top of Kid's head. "How long are you drafted for?"

"Two years," Luke said. He cleared his throat and glanced at Will before going on. "Seems like the weather might warm up soon. That's kind of nice."

Since Will wasn't going to allow them to discuss anything, Allison continued with the change in subject. "Do you mind if Kid plays with your dog?"

He looked surprised. "I didn't think about it, but I guess Georgie is mine now. Anyway... yeah, of course. There's a basket of toys around here someplace."

Luke got up and found the collection of toys meant for Georgie, producing a small tennis ball. "You want to play catch with Georgie?"

He was talking to Kid, but she remained motionless while Georgie's tail thumped at his leg. They went outside together, but Will shot Allison a look, and she knew exactly what he wanted. Will wanted to know why Luke hesitated when he answered that he was a nurse, so she was going to have to keep Luke busy for a little while.

.

13

A Match Made in Heaven

Harmon's Folly, Pennsylvania
February 29, 2020

Although it wasn't quite the end of winter and far too early for spring, the dandelions had already commenced their annual invasion of Aunt Cece's backyard. While there were only a few yellow heads to be seen, in a few months the lawn would be a thick yellow blanket. It was about a hundred yards from the rear of the house to the decrepit barn, and behind that they allowed the hay to grow as high as it wished. There was more than enough room to throw a ball around for an energetic border collie, with plenty of space left over.

Kid looked at the ball in her hand for a long time. Just when Luke was about to take it back and demonstrate how to throw it, Kid's arm darted back, and she lobbed it overhand across the yard.

Georgie transformed into a blur of black fur and pure ambition. Mission accomplished, he trotted back with the ball in his mouth, his tail wagging all the way. Instead of making Kid go through the rigamarole of stealing the ball back from him, Georgie dropped it in front of Kid's feet and then sat at attention, waiting for her to throw again.

"Oh, I see how it is," Luke told Georgie. The canine ignored him. He was the picture of focus—the ball had his full attention.

Allison clapped when Kid threw the ball a second time, all traces of her earlier anxiety departed. "You are so good at throwing!" she exclaimed.

Kid didn't pay any attention to the clapping or the compliment. She and Georgie were a match made in heaven; Kid threw and Georgie fetched—a relationship in such perfect harmony that Luke was envious.

"Maybe she played T-ball," Allison said to Luke. "Like with that stand and the plastic bat."

"Maybe." The dark cloud that had hung over them since their awkward hug, followed by the discussion in the basement, broke up, and rays of conversational sunshine returned.

"It's a game that I play," Allison said. "Where I make up a story about her from before, you know, everything. A good story. Something nice."

"Got it," Luke said. "Well, then... she definitely played baseball. I bet her team won the championship, and they got ice cream."

"Exactly! She was probably their best hitter."

"And the fastest runner," Luke added.

Allison laughed. "I believe that. I've seen her run."

"Well, then, she ran all the bases and won the game."

"Did you play baseball when you were a kid?" Allison asked.

"No. Football. What about you?"

"No. My brother did, though. For a couple years when we were real little. I remember going to the games."

"You have a brother?"

She nipped at her lip a moment before answering. "Had. He's dead."

"Was it from the Wormwood Prion?"

"No. He just finally got good at overdosing. Only took him a dozen times." She sighed and frowned. "We are losing this game."

Luke watched Kid throw the ball farther. "I would say she's definitely one of those sports prodigies you hear about."

"Her mom probably drove her all over to private T-ball coaches. I bet they cost a fortune," Allison said.

"They do. I had one."

"I thought you said you didn't play baseball?"

"Football. Pop was all about football. He hired a private coach to work with me during the off-season throughout high school."

She stared at him as if struggling to determine whether Luke was putting her on, and suddenly she laughed. "Yeah, right?"

"No, I'm serious," Luke said. "I did four years of year-round football."

"He paid for four years of that?"

"Yep. And it was a waste of money because I looked good in the uniform but not on the field. I ended up getting an academic scholarship, though, so it all worked out." Luke shrugged. "What about you? Did you do any sports in school?"

There was a loud bang behind them; Will stood in the grass just outside the back door. He whistled, provoking Luke's ire when Allison and Georgie turned to look at Will simultaneously.

He was about to say something sarcastic about Will when he spotted a blush creeping up the back of Allison's neck and dappling her cheeks. "I quit school, because my momma needed some help, and we were moving around a lot. But I wasn't into sports and all that stuff anyway, so it was fine."

Luke went to apologize, but she didn't give him a chance. "Since it turns out that you're a nurse, I'm guessing you know you shouldn't be around your aunt's body. Will and I will have to handle it."

"There's no evidence that you can pass prions after death."

"That's science talk for 'we don't know for sure,'" Allison said. "Why chance it?"

He couldn't argue with her logic, so he nodded.

"Can you stay with Kid and let her play for a while?"

Luke agreed, and after rubbing noses with Kid, she set off across the dandelion-spotted yard, picking her way around the low spots that were mushy from the thaw.

The sun was setting around the same time that Kid seemed to tire of throwing the ball for Georgie.

"Are you all done?" Luke asked her.

Kid wrapped her arms around his legs.

Luke didn't have cousins or younger siblings, so he wasn't sure what to do from there, but he couldn't walk with Kid holding his legs hostage. "How about a piggyback ride?" he offered.

She let go, which he assumed was an answer to his question, so he knelt down in front of her and waited for her to climb on. Apparently familiar with the concept of a piggyback ride, Kid slid her thin arms around his neck and held on. The moment the child grabbed onto him, Luke was transported away from Kid, Georgie, and the early spring of Aunt Cece's yard and straight into a nightmare: Timmy's chewed-up arms folded around his neck and the teeth that had hungered for Luke behind glass sinking readily into his tender neck—chewing, gnawing, boring into him. In the hospital, Luke had never heard Timmy speak, but in his nightmares, he had a voice, and he heard it there, in the yard.

Finally.

Luke recoiled, pitching them both forward. There was another moment of panic when her teeth accidentally grazed his shoulder. Luke recoiled again; he tried to stop himself, but his terror overruled his brain. He could tell that having her behind him where he couldn't see her was just going to keep triggering the same response, so he pushed her away gently while he flipped around so she was in front of him.

His face crimson, and shaken by both fear and embarrassment, Luke held out his arms to her. "Guess the piggyback ride broke down. How about if I just carry you?" he asked.

Timmy's cracked, guttural voice chuckled: *The better to see your teeth, my dear.*

14

Professional Grave Digger

Harmon's Folly, Pennsylvania
February 29, 2020

I f Kid understood or was bothered by what had happened, she gave no sign. When Luke picked her up, she laid her head on his shoulder and stuck her thumb in her mouth. Will and Allison had found shovels and were already digging a grave. When Luke reached them, he passed Kid over to Allison and took the shovel from her.

"Are you sure you're okay? Looked like you lost your balance out there," Will asked him, dryly.

Of course, Will had seen. And of course, Will had to say something in front of Allison about it. Luke really hated Will. Luke thrust his shovel into the ground. "Yeah, misjudged her weight is all."

"Really? Because you look a little spooked," Will said.

Allison gave a weary sigh. "I found some dish soap under the sink, and the hot water's working. I'm going to go give Kid a bubble bath. Do you two think you can handle this alone? Or should I stay and supervise?"

"Professional grave digger, darlin'," Will drawled with a smile.

"Yeah, right," Allison answered. "That does not count as my guess for today, by the way."

"Your guess?" Luke asked.

"Biters don't talk about before. It's a—" Allison's face scrunched up.

"Faux pas," Will finished.

"Yes," Allison said. "A faux pas. Except for what you did for work. But Will wouldn't tell anyone at the RC, and I'm only allowed to guess once a day."

"Shoot your shot," Will told her. "Sun's a sinkin'."

Allison made a show of thinking hard. "Hm... a shaman."

Will, the surly cuss who had been annoying Luke all day long, threw his head back and roared with laughter. "I can't believe you finally guessed it! I had the finest sweat lodge in the whole desert. You should have seen it."

"Used car salesman," Luke said loudly, without bothering to stop digging.

When no one answered, Luke looked Will in the eye. "Don't I get a guess?"

Will sucked his teeth and made a face like he'd tasted something sour. "Ladies only."

Luke knew he was right, and tried to keep from smirking but he failed, miserably.

"I don't know. That doesn't seem fair," Allison said to Will. "He ought to at least get one guess."

Luke continued to stare Will down.

"Well, them's the rules." Will shrugged and went back to digging. "And you already had your guess for today so you should probably go get that gremlin a bath."

Allison rolled her eyes and went into the house, the back door slamming shut behind her.

"You're scared of little girls," Will stated matter-of-factly. Will started digging faster, and Luke matched his pace.

"And you're a used car salesman chasing a girl a decade and a half younger than you," Luke replied. He dug faster than Will. Will narrowed his eyes and then matched Luke's pace.

"Oh, that's what you think. That I'm skirt-chasing?" Will answered.

"You're not?" Luke asked. "By the way, only old dudes like my pops say things like 'skirt-chasing.'"

"No. I am not. But it's not your business anyway, Normal," Will said.

"Because I didn't get infected, I can't have an opinion on you creeping on a girl young enough to be your—"

Will raised his shovel. "If you say daughter, I'll make this grave a double-wide."

Luke felt he might actually do just that, so he amended his statement. "Younger sister."

Will pursed his lips and resumed digging. "You can think what you want as long as you're staying away from her while you do it."

"I'm kind of busy burying my aunt and being drafted into the army right now, but even if I wasn't, she could decide for herself, couldn't she?"

"I found your employee badge while you were playing ball," Will said. "That's an awful lot of letters after your name, Doctor Wright."

Luke said nothing; he was too angry that Will had gone through his car and his things. He was regretting handing the gun back to Allison.

"Let me ask you something," Will said. "None of this ever happened, right? You're back home, maybe at a bar with your friends, and fate brings you face-to-face with my girl Al. What happens exactly, Doctor? Seems like a high school dropout from a Cincitucky trailer park slinging the drinks for you and your hoity-toity friends might be a bit below your standards."

"Dude, fuck you." Luke threw his shovel on the ground.

"No." Will stopped digging and dropped his own shovel. He pulled the gun from his waistband and stuck it in Luke's face. "Fuck you. You can't even see her, she's beyond your understanding."

"What the hell does that mean?"

"Let's just say she's got a certain skill set that needs encouraged, not stifled."

"I don't know what you're talking about, but I'm not fighting with you over some girl I'll probably never see again after tomorrow morning," Luke said. "But I will fight with you over the fact that I'm not some snobby asshole who would treat her like garbage. Whatever her skill set, she definitely deserves better than you."

Will lowered the gun from Luke's face and tucked it in his waistband before picking his shovel back up. "I said my piece."

"Yeah, sure, me too. Hey, Will, any idea where I can get a good deal on an Accord?"

"Fuck you, kid. Keep digging."

"Why don't you go inside? You look tired. I can take it from here."

"Not even a little bit tired."

"Really? Okay, cool. Thanks for the help."

Luke's muscles burned, but he didn't slow down. He was angry; with Will, with the fact that most of his family was dead, and with the world for having gone so off-kilter. Digging gave him a productive activity to channel, and he did that—the bonus was that Will couldn't keep up.

By the end, Luke had to give Will credit for helping until the grave was completely dug. Despite Will's protest that Luke should sit out and let Al help, they lowered his aunt into the grave together. Allison came out holding a still-damp Kid. Wrapped up in a towel, her head lying against Allison's shoulder, Kid sucked on her thumb and shut out the world. Allison held a bouquet of early tulips that Luke recognized from his aunt's front flower bed.

They had a crude funeral around his aunt's grave. Blistered hands and an aching back made it hard to concentrate, but he remembered a verse from a vacation bible school he'd attended in elementary school. Will recited an entire prayer from the Bible and paid homage to Aunt Cece with flourish and elegance. Afterwards, Allison set Kid down and handed her the flowers; unprompted, Kid tossed them on top of his Aunt Cece, making Luke wonder how many funerals Kid had attended.

Luke held out a blistered hand to Will. "Thank you for helping."

Will eyed it for a second and then took it. Luke expected a tighter-than-necessary squeeze, but it was a run-of-the-mill, firm handshake, and then Will went into the house, leaving Luke to fill the grave in alone.

Allison followed him inside, but after a couple of minutes she came out without Kid and picked up a shovel.

"You don't have to—" Luke began.

"I know," Allison said, and began shoveling dirt into the hole.

"Is Kid asleep?" Luke asked.

"Nah, we had to sleep together at the RC," Allison said. "So she's still used to that. She won't sleep until I go in."

"They didn't have enough beds?" Luke asked.

Allison bit her bottom lip: a telltale sign there was something she wasn't sure she should tell him. "Uh—no, it was just, um... safer that way."

Luke stopped digging, not sure what he was hearing. "Wait—you're talking about in the Recovery Centers?"

"After I met Will, it wasn't as much of an issue, but by then she was used to sleeping with me so we just kept that up."

They worked in silence for a few minutes, then Luke said, "My brother was in one in Nevada. He didn't live in Nevada. I'm not even sure how he ended up way over there."

She looked up at him. "He didn't survive the cure?"

"No, he did. He made it all the way through and got discharged. He died after that, and I can't get any answers about how and why. All I know is that it was blunt force trauma to the head and that it happened just outside of Vegas in the Relapse Riot," Luke said.

Luke glanced at Allison, who was biting her lip. "What?"

"Nothing," Allison said.

"I've watched the videos that leaked a hundred times. I just—was it just that one? Or were they all as bad as that?"

She shook her head slowly, her forehead creased in confusion. He'd forgotten; she didn't have any idea what videos he was talking about because they hadn't seen the news or been online in over a year. He wondered if she knew about Relapse Riots or what California had started.

"Never mind. But can you answer one thing?" Luke said. Allison looked wary. "How bad was it in the Center? I don't need details if you don't want to give them. On a scale of one to ten."

"Which is the worst?" Allison crinkled her nose.

"Ten."

She resumed shoveling. "A four."

"Really?" Luke asked. "That doesn't sound that bad."

"I mean, it sucks to have a forced routine and all. But it's not so bad. Kid sleeping with me was more of a precaution. In case she needed to go to the bathroom in the middle of the night or something. Didn't want her to get lost," Allison rambled on.

"I imagine your brother's Center was probably even better than mine was, being out west and all. Nice weather, lots of sunshine." She was lying to spare his feelings; rather than call her out, Luke nodded and kept working. When they finished, she asked him if he wanted to take the first shower, pointing out that it was his house. "Lady kidnappers first," he said. She gave him an exaggerated curtsy before disappearing into the house, while he went in search of a glass of water.

Twenty minutes later, she came downstairs with wet hair, fresh clothes, and bare feet. He headed up with his backpack; as he passed Allison in the kitchen, she glanced at it, which made him wonder if she'd been keeping him busy outside while Will rifled through his things. He checked it over carefully, but nothing was missing.

He took a fast shower, but it was fully dark outside by the time he finished. Will was asleep on the couch with a paperback novel covering his face. It was a long sofa, and Kid was curled up at the other end with her thumb in her mouth, and her eyes closed. He looked out the back kitchen door in time to see an Allison-shaped figure disappear into the dilapidated barn.

He found Allison sitting alone on the pine bench, which sat outside a stall that had belonged to a horse named Sal. Sal had died ten years ago, and Aunt Cece never got another horse because the idea of it broke her heart. She hadn't bothered to make repairs to the barn either, and most of the roof was missing, allowing silvery moonlight to filter down and illuminate the interior.

Allison looked up when he stepped into the barn. "Sorry, if I was intruding," she said. "At the TRC we were all together all the time. I was just trying solitude out to see how it fit."

"I can go," Luke said.

"Stay. I'm not sure being alone suits me anymore," she said.

"Kid looked like she was asleep," Luke said, sitting on the bench. "Will, too."

"Won't last long. She'll come looking for me pretty soon. We held you at gunpoint, and all that, but thanks for letting us borrow your house. Kid loved splashing in the tub."

"Thanks for making sure I didn't get myself killed. Or infected."

"Is that something you worry about? Getting infected?"

"Actually, no. I should worry, I guess. Most people do, according to my psychiatrist. But that's not the problem."

"What is the problem?"

"I just—I had an experience. And then after that we all locked down for a year. It's funny, but you guys are the first people I've been with since the hospital."

"I'll tell you a secret about getting infected."

"What's that?"

"It wasn't so bad, really."

"What?"

"Maybe it would be for you. But I didn't lose anything except all the bad stuff. I didn't have to worry about money and rent or my junkie father showing up to rip me off. All I worried about was pain and making it stop."

Luke didn't know what to say.

"Yeah, it sounds weird. But now I'm back and I have all the problems I had before, with even fewer ways to fix them. I worked three part-time jobs before I got sick. No one is going to hire Biters. Every business we passed had signs in the windows. They don't want our money—they definitely don't want to give us a job."

"Come with me to Cincinnati," Luke said. The idea had hit him in the shower, and he'd pushed the odd impulse aside immediately. However, sitting with her in the dark barn, it didn't feel like impossible brashness. It gripped him as an urgency, a thing that he absolutely must do without delay.

"What?"

"I'm serious. You and Kid should come with me. In fact, we can leave right now."

"And what about Will?"

"The hell with Will," Luke said. "You need to get away from him."

Allison rolled her eyes, stood up and walked to the barn door. "I'm going to bed."

Luke rose from the bench. "I'm serious. You'd be better off without him."

Allison raised an eyebrow. "Because you know so much about me and Will."

"He's a con man. And apparently a murderer, right? He killed someone yesterday."

"No, I killed someone yesterday. Will didn't get a drop of blood on himself."

"What?"

"That's right. He was going to shoot Will and Kid, and I would have been next. So I stabbed him. Over and over until I was sure he couldn't hurt us."

"Okay, well... you did what you had to do," Luke said. "But I also know that at some point, you're going to feel—"

"I don't."

"You don't what?"

"I don't feel anything at all. It didn't bother me one iota to kill him. In fact, I slept like a baby that night in the back seat of his car while I had his corpse stashed in the trunk a few feet behind me."

"Allison—"

"No. You don't know anything about me or Will, and you don't get to have an opinion on us."

"Fine, so you need some therapy. You've been through a horrible ordeal and—"

Allison laughed at him. "An ordeal? Some therapy? How do you think I got like this in the first place? That Doctor Harpy gave me so much therapy that I'm sick with it."

"Then you need real therapy. You're not some cold-blooded killer who—"

"You're right. I'm not a cold-blooded killer. But I am a killer, and that's a damn good thing because as it turns out, being cured is way more dangerous than being Infected ever was. And maybe you don't like Will, but he never acts like there's something wrong with me."

"I'm not trying to make you feel like there's something wrong with you. But what you described is textbook—"

Allison advanced on him with a murderous look in her eye. Luke instinctively backed away from her, but she kept coming until his back pressed against the rough-hewn boards that made up the barn walls, their faces inches apart.

"What's wrong, Luke? You seem a little anxious. Maybe even a little scared. Yet, you asked me to leave with you tomorrow. Which textbook covers this situation, exactly?"

She wasn't Allison. She was Al—the girl who belonged to Will and had held Luke pinned under her gaze in the car. Al, who had him pushed him aside to hunt down his aunt. Al, who had murdered a man yesterday and fallen asleep in his car with his body bleeding out in the trunk. When he didn't answer, she leaned forward, just short of her lips touching his. "Maybe you have a thing for danger. Is that it?"

"No." He finally found his voice. "I'm not scared of you."

"Are you sure about that?"

"I'm sure."

Her expression softened. "Then why? Why do you want me to come with you? Because you don't like Will?"

Luke could picture it in his head, and it seemed easy; he'd pack them up and drive away from Will. West seemed like a good idea. He'd drive them all the way to the Pacific Ocean and never look back.

"I won't be your excuse to dodge the draft. If you don't want to join the army, don't do it."

"That's not what it's about."

"It's not? Then tell me what it is about."

There was only one way to answer her. He kissed her. Instead of pushing him away or demanding to know why, she kissed him back. He knew she would never say yes and leave with him. He kept kissing her, anyway, determined to change her mind. She bunched the fabric of his shirt in her fists and pulled him closer to her, threw her arms around his neck.

His hands ran through her hair, skimmed across her shoulders, brushed down her back. He lifted her up, her legs wrapping around his waist while he spun them around until she was against the wall. She smelled like floral soap, and some other scent that was just her. Her arms had been loose about his neck, but she pulled him in tighter, harder. Kissing her felt like stepping off the edge of a cliff, knowing there was no going back. Instead of stopping, he just wanted more.

The sound of his pounding heart had muffled the first one, but the second gunshot coming from the house rang out loud and clear.

Allison's legs were still around him when the cold steel of a shotgun barrel pressed against the back of Luke's neck. "Drop the girl, nice and slow."

He let Allison down slowly and started to turn around, but something struck him in the back of the head, hard. He didn't realize he'd fallen down until Allison's head eclipsed the moon and she called his name.

He didn't lose consciousness, but it was a battle to stay awake. The man with the shotgun ordered them back to the house at gunpoint. Allison helped Luke walk; he tried to keep his weight off of her, but standing completely straight made the world spin in dizzying circles.

"Are you okay?" she whispered.

"No," he admitted.

"You prolly got a concussion. Let me do all the talking," she said.

"Shut up." The man with the shotgun bumped Allison's back with the barrel.

They were marched into the house through the back door, where another man with a full beard and shaggy hair was nursing his arm. Kid sat on the couch staring straight ahead, and Will was laid out on the floor, out cold.

"You see that dog out there?" the bearded man demanded. "Fucker bit me for grabbing the kid. I shot at him, but he ran off."

"You shot my dog?" Luke started, but he was tapped on the back of his head with the shotgun. Allison grabbed his hand and squeezed it.

"I sure hope so. Asshole dog..." he muttered.

"Let's load them up and take them to Clive."

15

Games of Chance

Before Wormwood, Clive Craig made Sales Associate of the Month six months running at the cell phone store he worked for. No one in the entire Midwest came close to Clive, a fact he bragged about often. Clive made lots of sales, but few friends, especially at work.

A lack of friends suited Clive fine. From an early age he'd learned that he'd have to wear a mask for the world, so the more often he was alone, the less he'd have to mask up to fit in.

Clive went through phases throughout his life; in high school he preferred pornography that featured older women; in his twenties he could only get off if some sort of animal was present; in his thirties, he became enamored of snuff films. It was a misconception, he discovered, that all snuff films featured some sort of sexual act, but quite accurate that immoral and salacious violence was its own special type of pornography. This realization led him to discover that anyone with vision and a camera could make those types of films.

Thanks to Wormwood, Clive simultaneously explored his newfound hobby of filmmaking and profited from it. He set up a private subscription service online and entertained his loyal subscribers with all manner of violently erotic short films. He had a standing order with a trio of idiots who brought him fresh actors for a free subscription to the channel.

Lately, poor Clive suffered from a lack of inspiration. Clive didn't realize it, but he wasn't in love with the films themselves anymore—it was the adoration of fans that revved his dopamine motor. He needed their adulation like he needed air; an endless cycle of theatre and applause that was difficult to maintain, and now, his window was closing.

Civility and law were creeping back into society, and he wouldn't be able to keep his backwoods project a secret for much longer. Clive wanted to go out with a bang: he had the script, he had the set, he had the vision—Clive just needed the right actors for the roles. Problem was, the only uninfected actors he safely got his hands on had been homeless people, and they weren't very appealing on camera. Then his beloved stooges brought Luke into his life—handsome, well-fed, and highly educated Luke. Clive's mouth watered.

Allison had never met Clive Craig before that day. When she looked at him, she saw a man who spoke softly, moved deliberately, and whose eyes lit up when he looked at Luke. Clive Craig scared the hell out of her—no small task, considering she was a monster herself.

She began at once. "He's a Normal, and he ain't with us. He's one of you. We kidnapped him."

"Is that so?" Clive asked. "Well, he seems in tip-top shape for a kidnapping victim."

"And he's drafted. And a doctor! That means the army will come lookin' if he doesn't report on time," Allison said.

Clive didn't like that.

"Didn't seem like much of a victim when you had your legs wrapped around him." The man who spoke up was Bill Thompson, a portly man on the downside of his forties, comfortably described as not very bright. He was neighbors with Aunt Cece and knew something was off when he noticed lights on inside the house, which prompted him to call up his friends to investigate. No one knew it, but he used to go there sometimes, and sit in the hallway outside her bedroom and torment poor Aunt Cece with his presence until he thought she might knock the doors off its hinges to get to him.

"Is that true?" Clive asked. Luke stared straight ahead, refusing to answer.

"Jealous?" Allison asked Bill. "I saw how you were looking at me in the truck."

Bill's face turned red. "I wasn't." He turned to Clive. "I ain't getting it with no Biter."

"Of course not, Bill," Clive said. He patted Bill on the shoulder. He used the same hand to backhand Allison across her mouth.

Allison spit the blood out and kept going. It was like poker, she figured, and Will had been exhaustive in his instruction about misdirection. Her goal was to keep them off-balance and sow doubt about Luke being a good hostage. If he could get free, he could bring back help.

"His draft papers are back at the house, if you don't believe me. I'm guessing he won't be too mad about the misunderstanding if you just let him go." Allison turned her attention to Bill. "And you, you liar. Why'd you have your hand up on my thigh, then?"

Clive hit her again. Her ears rang; she was going to have to be careful, or he'd knock her out. The last thing she wanted was to lose consciousness.

"Fine by me if you want the United States Army to come knocking," she said. "But if I were you, I'd let him go."

Clive crouched down in front of her, his boots scraping the gravel beneath them. "You're not me, though, are you? You are a freak. A walking disease who only exists because of a pansy-ass Congress who couldn't handle a little public backlash."

"Leave her alone," Luke said.

"The hero speaks," Clive said. "That's good. That's real good."

Clive made a frame out of the fingers of both hands and peered at Luke through it. "Is it true? Are you a doctor? Is the army going to come looking for you?" he asked.

Luke's jaw tightened up, and he went back to looking straight ahead, past Clive. He sighed and nodded at one of the men who had taken them from the house. He hit Luke between the shoulder blades with his shotgun, and then shoved Luke down to the ground, keeping one booted foot on his back to hold him still. "If you move, I shoot Blondie."

Clive stood up. "Take the little girl to school. Get that old man a nice seat at the roulette wheel."

Rough hands hauled her up to her feet; her arms were behind her back and her hands were zip-tied together at the wrists. Clive reached into another pocket and pulled out a long metal rod with leather straps and a buckle. Allison fought back by turning her head away and keeping her mouth closed, but they held her head still, and Clive pinched her nose closed until she had no choice but to gasp for air. He shoved the long piece of metal into her mouth and between her teeth, and Bill buckled it behind her head. It rested uncomfortably against her tongue, and she could taste old copper pennies and something acrid and awful that she couldn't identify. She wanted to retch.

"That's better," he said. "You don't have any lines in this film. You're just going to scream. Don't worry, you'll know when."

Clive climbed into the cab of a brand-new pickup truck; Bill dragged Allison inside to ride shotgun. The remaining men marched Luke to the back of the truck and put him into the bed. Clive drove them down a narrow gravel driveway, dimly lit by mismatched patio lanterns through the branches of the trees. Eventually, they came to a clearing and the remnants of an enormous bonfire. Their destination lay on the other side of the charred logs.

It was an old elementary school, and it was having a carnival.

It was a far different carnival than Allison remembered from her childhood. That had been a pleasant daytime affair put on by the PTA to raise money for some noble cause. There had been music, food, games, and fun.

Clive's carnival was a sinister event held under the light of a full moon. He parked the truck in front of the first booth and got out. Bill was still sore that she'd outed him for touching her, so he wasn't very gentle with Allison when he pulled her out of the truck. He yanked as she was stepping out, and she fell to the ground, earning skinned knees. Bill laughed when he saw the blood, but Clive scowled and said that Bill should be more careful with the talent. Allison made a face at Bill, and while he couldn't hit her, he grabbed ahold of her arm and squeezed his fat fingers into the soft flesh of her bicep hard enough to bring tears to her eyes.

Clive reached out and flipped a switch. Bright light washed over the booth, provided by a spotlight in one corner of the booth, a camera suspended in the opposite corner.

"You missed the big party. Lucky for you, we haven't cleaned up yet." Clive offered her a dart. "Take your shot, miss."

Balloons filled the board, but every third balloon was missing. A cutout oval with a Biter's face was in its place. Their jaws opened and closed at the sound of Clive's voice. Allison shook her head, refusing to play.

"How silly of me. I forgot to offer the prize. No reason to play a game if there isn't a prize, right?"

"Fuck you," Allison said, but it sounded like "Uck ooo." Clive, having played many games with many people, knew what she meant.

"If you can get fifty points with two darts, I'll let you go."

Allison studied the board. Small cards assigned every Biter points, marking how many points they were each worth. Based on what she saw, she'd have to make both darts on her first try in order to win.

She tried to ask a question.

Clive frowned. "I didn't quite catch that."

Allison repeated the question. He sighed and reached around to the back of her head, unlatching the strap, freeing the bit from her mouth. She spit it out, but he caught it smoothly before it could fall to the ground.

"I said, how much do those two darts cost me?"

The corners of his mouth curled up into a smirk. "You're the first person to ask me that."

"That's how it works, right? Two darts for five bucks or whatever. Then I win a prize that's not even worth the price of the darts. Even if I make the shots, what good is letting me go going to do? I'm not leaving without my kid."

"Two darts for two fingers. I'll let you choose which fingers, though," Clive said conversationally.

"How about one finger, I still pick which one, and we skip the darts? You just let my kid go."

"Without the game, there's no show. Without the show, I'm a broke lunatic running a weird carnival," Clive said.

"I'm not playing any games that I don't have a chance of winning," Allison said.

"That's not a very inspired attitude," Clive said. He pushed her hair away from her face; she tried to duck away but failed. "Let's try again."

"Don't touch her," Luke said. He was rewarded with another blow to the back.

Clive regarded Luke carefully. "Tough guy. I've got just the game for you."

He walked them to a game she recognized as a way to test strength. The player was meant to use the large mallet to hit the lever hard enough to cause the puck to rise high enough on the long pole to ring a bell at the top.

Clive held out the mallet to Luke, who didn't accept it. Clive gave a nod to Bill, who grabbed Allison's hands, which were tied behind her back. The sharp edge of a knife bit into her thumb, and she cried out.

"I won't kill her, but I will start taking parts off of her. I really need you to get your head in the game, soldier."

Luke took the mallet. "What do I get if I ring the bell?"

"You get to leave."

"What about them?" Luke asked.

Clive shrugged. "What about them? I thought they kidnapped you and held you against your will." There were some snickers between Bill and his friends.

"What if I don't ring the bell?" Luke asked.

Clive grinned a toothy smile. "Then you stay, and we have some fun."

Luke gripped the mallet and without looking away from Clive, weakly hit the lever, barely moving the puck.

Clive gave a deep and weary sigh. "I just don't think either of you are embracing the spirit of my games of chance."

"Maybe because we can't win jack shit," Allison said.

"Freedom? I offered you each your freedom."

"For one of us. We're supposed to leave the rest behind? No thanks," Luke said.

Clive chewed on the inside of his lip, thinking. "Well, I think I've got just the game for this situation."

Allison and Luke shared a look; neither of them liked the sound of that.

The temperature had dropped considerably, and clouds moved in and covered the moon. Allison was breathing hard, from anticipation and fear, and her breath made little puffs in the air.

"You played football, right? It can't be much harder than throwing a football. I mean, you need aim for that."

"I was the kicker. And I told you, I wasn't that great," Luke said.

"Kicker? No offense, but that sounds pretty useless right now."

Clive tossed a softball to Luke, who nearly dropped it.

"Yep," Luke agreed. "You definitely should have kidnapped Roger Parsons."

"Who's that?"

"The quarterback of the team. He also slept with my prom date."

"Roger sounds like a dick, but I do kind of wish I'd kidnapped him instead."

"Do I get a practice throw?" Luke asked Clive.

Clive's eyes lit up; he was pleased that they were accepting the challenge and playing the game. "Yes. Go."

Luke threw the softball as hard as he could and missed the target by at least four feet.

"Luke? Whatever happens. Let it go."

"What?"

"I don't know what happened to you." Bill started to drag Allison away. She dug in her heels so she could get her say. "But don't hold on to this like you were holding on to that. You hear? If you make it out, just let it go."

Clive and company had modified a dunking tank. Someone with a penchant for carpentry had built a wooden platform next to the tank. Atop that platform was a cage. Inside the cage was an extremely agitated Infected.

The top of the tank was also modified. A chair sat on a platform, and if Luke successfully hit the target, the platform would open up, drop Allison into the tank, and then close again. Clive had already demonstrated the mechanism when he explained the rules.

They put the bar back into Allison's mouth and buckled it up in the back so she couldn't speak. They sat her down in the chair, drizzled some blood from a bucket on the wood between her and the Infected, and left her alone.

Clive pulled on a chain, and the cage door lifted two inches. The Infected tried to shove his face underneath and howled in frustration at being denied.

"Your move."

Luke picked up a softball from the small basket in front of him. He took a deep breath and concentrated on the target, before throwing as hard as he could. It was a considerably better throw than his test one had been, but he still missed the target by a foot.

Clive pulled the chain, and the cage door lifted up by a few more inches.

"One down, two to go."

Luke selected another ball. This time he took three deep breaths to calm himself before throwing the ball. He missed by two feet, at least.

Clive pulled on the chain, and the door lifted up a few more inches. The Infected shoved eager hands underneath and tried to reach Allison; his fingers drifted across the top of her feet. She squeezed her eyes shut and shouted to Luke. "Promise me you'll get Kid out."

"One more," Clive said.

Luke's hands were shaking. His terrible aim was going to get Allison killed in the slowest, most horrifying way imaginable. He tried not to think about it; like she'd said, he had to let it go. At least for right now, so he could concentrate on throwing the ball.

"Ticktock."

He'd already missed two throws, three if he counted the practice throw, and it was clear that deep breathing was not remotely helpful to him in this particular circumstance. While he had never played baseball on a team, he'd played catch with his brother in the yard plenty of times, and he tried to think about that. The target was Mark's glove, and all he had to do was throw the ball into Mark's glove, which he'd done a hundred times as a kid.

No big deal.

Luke closed his eyes a moment and pictured his brother's face. He envisioned Mark standing there, with his glove up, waiting on Luke to throw the ball.

Let's go, Luke. I'm not getting any younger.

Luke opened his eyes, and still trying to keep the picture of his brother in his head, he hurled the ball at the target.

He struck it dead center. The platform under Allison swung, and a surprised and muffled scream rang into the night, immediately followed by a splash.

"I did it," Luke said in awe.

Clive nodded slowly and licked his lips.

"We had a deal," Luke reminded him. "Get her out."

"Do it," Clive said to Bill, who looked dejected. He stomped to the tank and started the process of fishing out Allison. It was awkward for him; she couldn't help with her hands tied behind her back, and by the time he got her out, he was panting hard.

Clive fiddled with the chains, and the cage door slammed down, landing on top of the Infected's hands. He howled in pain, and Clive went up and adjusted the cage manually, kicking the hands back under the door. Bill brought Allison to Luke. With each violent shiver, more water dripped and fell to the ground. She hadn't been out of the tank long, but her lips had already lost their color and were well on their way to turning blue.

"Untie her," Luke said to Bill.

Bill looked to Clive, who came forward with a small pocketknife. He handed it over to Bill, presumably to cut the zip tie around Allison's wrists. Bill held on to the knife but didn't move.

"You won, fair and square," Clive said. He extended his hand to Luke to shake it.

"Untie her," Luke said, refusing to take it.

"C'mon. No need to be rude," Clive said. "Especially with a knife this close to your girlfriend."

With no choice, Luke took Clive's offered hand. Clive yanked him in close very quickly, kicked his legs out from under him, and pushed him to the ground. Luke's face was pressed against mud and gravel before he had time to think about what had just happened. Clive had the element of surprise, but Luke was stronger, and he used his body to push himself up, which worked—until he felt the sharp prick of a needle in his neck.

The effect was immediate. Clive let go of him, but Luke couldn't force his limbs to cooperate enough to get up off the ground, and he ended up collapsing in a heap. Before everything went dark, he heard Clive speak one last time.

"You know, for a doctor, you're kinda dumb."

16
VIP

Harmon's Folly, Pennsylvania
March 1, 2020
396 days post-WPE

They took Luke away, but wouldn't tell her where. Clive removed her gag, which meant he was either going to do something to make her scream or make weird idle small talk, both of which turned her stomach.

"What was in that needle?" she asked.

"Did you really kidnap him?" Clive asked.

"Yes."

"If someone kidnapped me, I don't think I'd care if they lived or died, but he was awful worried about you."

"I'm a really good kidnapper," Allison said.

Clive was entertained; he desperately hoped everything would play out on screen the way he was imagining it—a magnum opus to retire on.

"So am I," Clive said. Her hair was a distraction; he pushed it out of her eyes again. "I can't wait to show you how good."

Clive paraded her past his morbid carnival games and out the other side until they reached a pole building. Clive unlocked the padlock with a set of keys from his pocket and let them both inside. The smell hit her as soon as she stepped inside: rotted meat, filth, and death. She recoiled; Clive noticed.

"What's wrong there?" he asked.

"Nothing."

"Nothing? Listen here, sugar, one thing I can't abide is a liar."

Allison turned her face away from him. She found it hard to believe that he couldn't smell the odors in the building, but he seemed completely oblivious to them. He flipped a switch, and several overhead lights came on.

He seized her chin and forced her to face him. "I want to show you something."

They dragged Allison through the building, past a monitoring station that featured at least a dozen monitors and a multitude of sophisticated-looking computer equipment. He halted and pointed to one monitor. They had strapped Will down to a giant wheel; a man wearing a clown costume threw a large butcher knife while the wheel turned, missing Will's head by inches.

"That's Bubbles. He's pretty good with knives. He'll keep the action going for the subscribers until at least dawn."

"Subscribers?" Allison asked. She searched the monitors for some sign of Kid or Luke.

"People pay good money to watch Biters 'bite it.' Pardon the pun," Clive said.

"That's what this is? That's what all the cameras are for? You charge people to watch you kill us?" Allison asked.

"Sure do. I take requests, too," Clive said proudly. "Of course, your friend messed things up a bit when he actually hit the target. That entire segment is useless now. People don't tune in to see you win, you know."

On a screen in the lower left, she saw a room lit in night vision mode that had several figures in it. Most weren't moving, but there was a heap in the middle that might have been Luke.

"What requests?" she asked. She needed to stall him longer, until she found Kid.

"It's not like some country came in and invaded us. Our loved ones attacked us. During a fiftieth anniversary party. Baby's bath time. Passionate sex. People are broken and angry, and there's no one to take it out on. Billy Bob in Kansas can't get over his best friend killing his fiancée because the best friend is as dead as the fiancée. So for my VIP customers, I find a Biter who looks close to the best friend and illustrate a carefully orchestrated demise that gives poor Billy Bob some closure."

Allison scanned the screens again. She couldn't find Kid.

"Sounds like you're doing the Lord's work."

Clive chuckled. "This has got nothing to do with the Lord. I'm just a businessman filling a need. One that I can relate to."

Clive took her arm and pulled her away.

"Hold on, where is my little girl?"

Clive glanced at the monitors. "Don't worry. It's all in the script. We're giving Romeo a situation he should be able to escape from, easily enough. And if not, we'll help him and nudge him along. He will save the little girl, and then they will come here. To try and save you."

"But you just said no one wants to see—"

Clive pulled her away. "Worry about yourself."

They walked to a corner of the warehouse that was dimly lit by the overhead lighting. Clive flipped switches until dozens of bright lights illuminated the corner.

There was a king-sized bed, with a mirrored ceiling, and a body hung where the headboard might be. Allison guessed the corpse to have been a woman, but advanced decomposition obscured any defining features, and a tattered silk nightgown still clung precariously to the cadaver. Large dog kennels stood off to the side—they each held a Biter.

The Biters reached through the bars, frantic for something to chew on. These were not the half-starved Biters. Just like the one at the dunk tank, they were strong—Clive had been feeding them.

"I normally shoot at the school, but I've been saving this stage for something special. You and that boy are going to be a perfect fit for this."

Clive gestured to the carcass at the head of the bed. "Her name was Eileen. She was pretty. Charming. A real head-turner."

Clive pulled her towards the bed. Allison planted her feet, but Clive's lackeys grabbed her from behind and dragged her the rest of the way.

Clive gestured at the kennels. "These are the four guys she was having intercourse with behind my back."

They forced Allison into a sitting position at the end of the bed, and Clive sat next to her.

"I was a great friend. I was trying out, you know, for the boyfriend position. I bought her nice things, listened to all her problems. But it didn't matter. She didn't see me. I wasn't her type."

Allison wiggled her wrists around in circles to test the binds. The zip ties cut into her skin. "You got friend-zoned." She hoped she sounded sympathetic.

"Exactly," Clive said. "So one day I decide to just show up and put it all out there. It's the apocalypse, right? No time like the present. I have a key to her place, so I let myself in and there's ole Gary, our manager at the store, chomping away on her intestines. She was looking right at me. Her lips were moving, but no sound was coming out. I assume she wanted me to help her, and I was going to, but then I realized Gary had his shirt off and his jeans down round his ankles. Do you know what I did next?"

"I have absolutely no idea," Allison said. She wriggled her wrists harder, hoping she'd loosen them enough to get free.

"I pulled up a chair and watched. It was a transformative experience—live just like on Broadway. Afterwards, I used her phone to track down the rest of her little playmates. But I've always regretted that I didn't have the presence of mind to record her and Gary together, and well, now here we are."

Allison suddenly saw where he was going with his speech and went to jump up, but Clive grabbed her arm firmly and plunged a syringe into her neck, the same way he'd done to Luke.

"You're going to help recreate this scene for my audience. When your boyfriend makes it out of the school, he's going to come here to rescue you and find you being eaten alive by Gary, just like I found my beautiful Eileen. Like I said, I'm filling a need for the customer, one that I keenly understand. Tonight, I am the VIP."

Luke woke up in the pitch black.

"Welcome back, Private."

Luke, still groggy from whatever they had injected him with, tried to find the owner of the voice. Or see anything at all. But it was too dark.

"It's time for the next game. You've heard of bobbing for apples?"

Luke recognized the creepy, slow cadence of Clive's voice. He tried to get to his feet; his gut roiled and threatened to overturn its contents at any moment.

"In case you haven't—a bunch of nice crisp apples are dumped into a barrel of cold water. You dunk your head into the water and try to grab an apple with just your teeth."

Instead of responding, Luke concerned himself with remaining steady on his feet. A powerful growl behind him broke the silence, and he whirled around to face it.

"You're the apple. You're going to bob around in the dark while teeth try to snatch you up. How many Biters? Could be one. Could be twelve."

The voice was coming from up high; it was a speaker he was hearing. Luke shook his head to clear it while chains rattled in the void.

"Looks like everyone's awake now," Clive went on. "If you make it out of that room alive, you can come get Blondie. She was pretty concerned about—well... she's not too worried about anything right now. I don't want to alarm you, but Blondie will not be with us much longer. Good luck, soldier."

Luke held still and stayed quiet. The Infected growled and rattled chains, hoping to get free. He couldn't guess how many; the rattling and other noises blended together into a cacophony of violent promises.

He should move, he knew. Any direction was better than staying put, but he didn't want to walk straight into the jaws of the Infected. He strained to see something; he would have settled for a shadow, but it was absolutely pitch black.

He had to stay calm because panic would get him killed. He took a deep breath, and then exhaled slowly, using every tool in his therapist-provided arsenal to not run screaming in any direction. It was improbable that he could navigate the room without getting bitten, so he considered how to protect himself. Most of the wounds he'd treated were defensive. His shirt was too thin to offer much protection, but his jeans might do the trick.

Luke quickly dropped his jeans and then folded them in half before wrapping the fabric around his left arm. From there he held that arm out in front of his face, elbow out, and kept his right hand balled into a fist, ready to deliver a right hook, if needed.

He was going to die.

Luke closed his eyes and took another deep breath. He couldn't die. From the sound of it, Clive had engineered something that gave Luke a chance to rescue Allison. If he died, she died. And Kid and Will. He had to keep it together and get out of there.

Luke took another step forward. He remembered the soldier who'd helped him ease his way out of the hospital.

Just one step. Then one more.

That was all he had to do. Take a step, stop, and listen.

Luke took another step; hot, stinking breath breezed against his right ear. He recoiled and moved left. A cry filled the room, angry over being denied a meal.

Luke was too close to it for comfort, and he hoped the chains were sturdy. He moved left again, his arm out, ready to catch teeth if needed. His eyes continued to strain against the darkness, desperate to see a hint of anything.

It was useless; the blackness enveloped him. He struggled to find the Infected he'd accidentally gotten too close to, but not even a shadow would reveal itself. He couldn't rely on hearing either, because the chains rattled in the dark, muffling any breathing or movement that Luke might have been able to pick up on.

Luke swung his wrapped arm in front of him and took one more step.

Something seized him in the darkness.

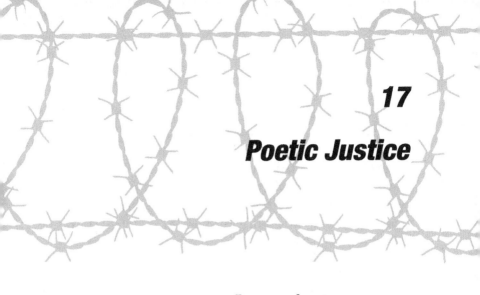

17

Poetic Justice

Harmon's Folly, Pennsylvania
March 1, 2020
396 days post-WPE

Allison returned to wakefulness in fits and starts. The drug kept pulling her back down, but she bobbed back up to the surface of consciousness. A growl accompanied a puff of hot breath against the sole of her right foot. When she tried to jerk her foot away, she couldn't—she was flat on her back, her arms and legs tied down.

Throwing her head back, she looked at the ceiling and didn't fully comprehend what she saw in the mirror there. At first, the only thing that registered was the color red. Then she understood that she was the red thing—covered in blood from head to toe. Panicked, she shrieked, looking for her mortal injury in the mirror, assuming that Clive's Biter had feasted on her while she was unconscious.

Clive laughed. "It's not your blood. You Biters prefer not to eat your own kind, so I got creative. Sort of like dressing up the broccoli with some chocolate sauce for a picky child."

Clive had Gary, the mobile-store-manager-turned-Biter, at the end of a long pole, a setup similar to what animal control used on stray dogs. Clive held him at bay, just inches away from her feet. Gary wore a full-face metal grid mask, his hands bound behind his back.

The Biter strained against the pole, nostrils flaring, teeth clacking. "Looks like it's working."

Clive let the Biter go, and he was on top of Allison, teeth gnashing uselessly behind the metal bars of the mask, embedding the metal into her body to try to get a bite of her. She didn't want to give Clive the satisfaction of a reaction, but she couldn't help it; she screamed and cried and tried to buck Gary off of her. The mask was homemade, and the steel had rough edges; it cut her all over, mingling her own blood with the uninfected blood that Clive had gotten from who-knew-where.

Gary was feral. Furious at being denied a meal, he wailed and howled at her, spittle hitting her in the face. She looked him in the eye, mesmerized momentarily by the terrible sight of him—visceral pain and hunger, which had once been her own. Until that moment, she hadn't known what she had looked like when she was infected: she'd been ugly; she'd been terrifying; she'd been powerless—just as powerless as she was now.

Gary stopped screaming and looked back into Allison's eyes just as Clive pulled him off her. "Screen test is over. This is going to be a fantastic shot."

Allison willed her body to stop trembling, caught her breath, and scrambled to think fast.

"It would be a better shot if I wasn't tied to the bed," Allison said.

Clive chuckled at her while he wrangled control of the Biter.

"I'm serious," Allison said. "Was Eileen tied to her bed?"

She had Clive's attention.

"I'm gonna die here. I know that," she said.

Clive handed his Biter over to one of his men, came over to the side of the bed, and sat down. His cloying, cheap cologne threatened to suffocate her. "I know what you're trying to do, but you can't get away."

"I never asked to catch Wormwood. But I also never asked to be cured. This world fucking sucks, and I want off. Getting killed by another Biter seems... poetic or something. If I'm going out, it might as well be a good show. Something that people will remember."

He cocked his head, intrigued. "What are you thinking?"

"I could try to fight him off. I can't win because he's bigger and stronger than me, but your subscribers will like that better than me just lying here like a dead fish."

Clive stroked his chin.

"Me fighting back will make him more violent, too."

She had him. His eyes glazed over, black pupils threatening to consume the brown of his irises completely as he pictured her violent demise.

"The only thing that I want—"

"Ah, there it is," Clive said.

"Let my kid go. You do that and you'll have a great show."

"Is she even your kid? She doesn't look like you."

"Yes, she is."

"What about the old man?"

"What about him? He's the one who insisted we had to come to fucking Pittsburgh in the first place."

Clive's lips twisted up, the happy ghoul.

"And your boyfriend? You don't want to make a deal for him?"

"That's a waste of time. You're never going to let either of us go. I just want my little girl to make it out alive. Do we have a deal?"

"I think we might."

"I want to see her."

Clive's smile faded. "I'm on a schedule here, sugar."

"If you want me to give a motivated performance, then I need to know she's going to go free. Sugar."

Clive stood up and paced next to the bed for several minutes. Eventually he stopped and leaned over the bed to her, both of his palms planted firmly on the bloodied bedspread, his single earring glinting in the stage lights.

"It's a deal."

Luke yelled and propelled himself backwards; in doing so, he landed squarely in range of the Infected he'd nearly walked into moments before. He heard it just in time to bring his wrapped arm up to defend himself. Teeth bore down hard on his denim-clad arm, locking his forearm between the Infected's jaws like a vise. He tried to regain his footing and wrench his arm free, but the Infected held fast and continued to bite down. Luke panicked that it was going to tear right through the denim and into his arm, and he planted his feet and pulled as hard as he could.

The denim wasn't enough for it to hold on to, and the fabric shifted in its mouth, sliding free, and Luke fell backwards and landed on the floor, hard.

Tiny hands grabbed him instantly, and Luke recoiled again, but the hand pressed something round and rough at him. He grabbed it with his hands.

It was a tennis ball.

"Kid?" Luke asked. "Is that you?"

A small hand grabbed his and held on.

Luke pulled her close to him and lifted her up. He hugged her tightly. "How did you get in here? Are you okay?"

Her head lay against his chest, and he heard the distinct sound of a thumb being sucked.

"I don't suppose you have any idea how to get out of here."

Kid's head lifted off his chest, and she wiggled her body to be set down. Once Luke complied, she grabbed his hand and tugged.

"Wait, really? You can see?"

She tugged at his hand again.

"Hold on," Luke said. He dropped to his knees. "Kid, do you know where Allison is?"

Small hands grabbed each side of his face, and they forced his head up and down in a nodding motion.

Luke stood up. "Let's go get her."

"Can I use the bathroom?"

Clive laughed at her.

"I'm serious. I gotta pee."

"I absolutely don't care."

Allison huffed. "I'm supposed to die with a full bladder? How the hell am I gonna fend off an attack when all I'm thinking about is how I need to pee?"

Clive tinkered with his camera some more. "It's a problem that you'll only have to worry about for sixty more seconds. It's time to get started."

"Whoa, we had a deal! I get to see my kid and know she's getting released."

"About that. I've changed my mind on a few things," Clive said.

Allison blanched. "Such as?"

Clive undid the restraint on her left wrist, careful to stay out of her reach while he did so. He walked around to the left leg and undid the restraint on her left ankle. "I don't think it's wise to leave you completely unfettered, as it were."

Clive whistled, and Bill removed the Biter from his cage. Together, they removed the mask and used the pole to position him at the foot of the bed. Clive turned back to Allison and briskly undid the restraint on her right wrist.

"The little girl is slippery and awful good at moving around in the dark. She shimmied her way through an air vent and waltzed right in and found your lover boy before we even started adding some light into the room for him to see by. They'll be here shortly, a little ahead of schedule, but we'll roll with it."

Clive whistled again, and a voice called back that they were rolling.

"Action!"

Clive backed away from the bed in three quick paces, and Allison sat up and started working on the last restraint on her right ankle. Bill fumbled with the pole a bit, but after a second, Gary launched himself at her on the bed.

Allison had no choice but to abandon her pursuit of freedom in favor of defending her life. She grabbed the leather cuff that had held her left ankle and stuffed it into his mouth and used her arms to hold him back. Will had told her a hundred times at the RC what to do in her situation.

If things go sideways, you just stall until I get there.

But they weren't in the RC anymore, and she was completely out of stalling time. Allison began screaming for Will as loud as she could; her terror reverberated through the warehouse and mixed with Clive's barking laughs. Gary fought back, jaws scissoring in ravenous anticipation of flesh, and she focused all her strength on holding him at bay and keeping the strap stuffed in his mouth. Her arms pushed against his face and chest, every fiber of her being straining with the effort of keeping his teeth away from her body.

Allison saw herself reflected in Gary's dark pupils—she was as wild and desperate to survive as Gary was to chew through her. Gary could be cured; she could smell it underneath all the other odors of extended captivity. They weren't different at all, she thought wildly—they were the same. She'd been trying to get into Clive's head before, but maybe it would be poetic justice for Gary to kill her. Struck by the impulse to lie back and stop fighting, she wondered how long it would take to die.

Gary stopped lunging at her. His head pitched forward, then he inhaled deeply and gave a low growl. He sniffed her again, nostrils flaring, lifted his head towards the ceiling, and let out a frustrated howl of anger. Apparently, Clive's ruse of covering her in uninfected blood had run out of steam.

Gary, completely unencumbered for the sake of exciting television, sniffed the air wildly. He zeroed in immediately on Bill, scrambled on all fours with astonishing speed, and launched himself at his new prey.

Screams and satisfied grunts filled the air while Allison shot up to sitting and began fumbling at the buckle on her restraints once more. Clive, unconcerned about his compatriot being eaten alive, turned his attention to Allison and punched her squarely in the mouth. She dropped backwards on the bed, dazed; something fell and struck her in the face. Her ears rang and, still stunned, she brushed her face with her hand. Her fingers closed around something—it was a piece of bone. The decomposed and brittle corpse had rained down on her from above, the eternally watchful Eileen solemnly presiding over the morbid affair. The bone had carried small bits of matter with it, and Allison blinked, spit, and wiped at her face to keep it from getting into her eyes and mouth.

Clive jumped on her and straddled her waist, his hands around her throat, and he began squeezing, berating the long-dead Eileen the entire time. Allison beat at his chest with a useless fist while she used the other to try and find the bone she had dropped when he leaped on top of her.

Black dots began swimming across her view of Clive's hateful reddened face when something hit Clive in the back of the head. Clive, stunned, stopped strangling Allison to see what had hit him. Allison choked, sputtered, and when she had his attention again, drove the long thin shard of bone directly into Clive's right eye.

Clive screamed, and Allison bucked and shoved at him, knocking him off of her. He rolled to the side, still screaming, holding his hands just shy of the object, afraid to touch it. Allison sat up in time to catch sight of Luke and Kid at the other cage next to Gary's empty one. While she unfastened the restraint that held her to the bed, Luke opened the cage, hastily hiding behind the door as it swung wide to let the Biter out.

The Biter made a beeline for Clive; he wasn't in danger of being bitten, courtesy of the homemade mask, but the grappling that ensued did little to help Clive's gentle treatment of the long piece of bone sticking out of his eye.

As soon as the Biter had run from the cage, Luke swung it shut and ran to Allison. She was still wheezing and gagging from Clive's attempt to choke the life out of her, trying to crawl away on her own. Luke lifted her off the bed. He intended to carry her out, but Allison patted his arm and asked him, in a hoarse croak, to let her down and take Kid instead.

The three of them gave Gary a wide berth on their way to the front door and were nearly there when a gunshot reverberated through the building. Allison and Luke dropped instinctively and looked around.

Clive had shot the Biter that had attacked him, and he was advancing on them with the gun. They bolted for the door. Clive took a shot at them, and Allison screamed when something whizzed by her ear. They ran out the door into the impending dawn, the cold prickling at Allison, who was still wet from her dunking and subsequent bloodbath.

An old pickup truck was barreling towards them, headlights bouncing on the rough terrain. They froze a moment, thinking their escape attempt was over; the truck came to a skidding stop just a few feet from them.

Will was in the driver's seat. Blood oozed from various parts of his upper body, and his teeth were bloodstained when he painfully smiled at Allison. "Going my way?"

They piled inside the cab of the pickup truck, Luke not able to shut the door completely before Will gunned the engine. Clive ran after them and fired the gun until he was out of bullets. Allison turned to watch Clive out of the back window, just in time to see Gary run out of the building behind Clive and take him down to the ground.

"Is anyone hit?" Will asked.

Kid was on Luke's lap, and Allison quickly checked her over, but she seemed fine. Kid wrapped her arms around Luke, laid her head across his chest, sucked her thumb, and closed her eyes.

"You all right?" Will asked Allison.

She didn't know. Her hands were shaking, so she shoved them under her legs to hide them. She might cry if she answered him out loud, so she just nodded and bit at the inside of her lip.

When they got to the end of the gravel road, Will turned sharply onto the paved highway. The truck lurched wildly to one side, and it pitched Allison against Luke. She had to pull her hands out from under her legs to keep from falling on top of him, and Luke grabbed one hand and asked her again if she was okay.

She nodded again; she could tell Luke didn't believe her, but hoped that he wouldn't ask again. They drove to Luke's Aunt Cece's house, Allison focused on keeping herself together the entire way. She tried not to think about Gary on top of her, or almost dying, or worse, almost giving up. She must have squeezed Luke's hand at some point because he squeezed it back twice to get her attention, and though he didn't ask her out loud if she was okay, his eyes said it all. When Will turned into Aunt Cece's driveway, she finally noticed something.

"Luke, why are you wearing your pants around your arm?"

18

Sugar

Harmon's Folly, Pennsylvania
March 1, 2020
396 days post-WPE

"Grab your stuff. We're leaving," Will said, before getting out of the truck. He pointed at Luke. "You, too. You get on the interstate and don't look back."

"What about the police? We should—"

"The police? A small town like this? Pretty sure they know exactly what was going on back there," Will said.

"You think they were in on it?" Luke asked.

"He made a lot of money killing and torturing Biters like us," Allison said. "Enough to pay people off and plenty left over."

Kid stirred in Luke's arms. He waited a second for her to settle back down to sleep before going on in a lowered voice. "We can't let him, or them, get away with this."

"I'm not sure he's even alive. Gary jumped him while we were driving away," Allison said quietly.

"Who's Gary?" Luke asked.

"He's the Biter that was supposed to be killing me when you walked in. Clive had it all planned out. You were supposed to come in with Kid, thinking you could save me, and it was supposed to be too late." She turned to Will. "Gary was a good guppy."

Will nodded that he understood; his jaw set in a hard line, brow worried.

She looked at Luke, her voice flat. "Eileen liked Gary better than Clive."

"Okay," Luke said. "Sounds like... you got to know Clive." He looked to Will for some sort of sign about what to do next, but Will just shook his head.

"C'mon, Al. We need to get out of here."

She nibbled at her lip a little before taking a deep breath and putting out her arms for Luke to hand Kid over.

He didn't want to. Not yet. "I can carry her in for you."

She looked like she might argue, but changed her mind. She slid across the bench seat and got out of the driver's side, leaving Luke and Kid alone in the truck. She and Will disappeared through the front door together.

Kid sat up and looked around.

"Hey, kiddo," Luke said. Kid looked up at him, her big owl eyes placid, as if they had not just all narrowly escaped with their lives.

"I wanted to tell you that when we were playing outside earlier, I got spooked. But it had nothing to do with you. Okay? I—I've been feeling guilty about some things and... well, none of that has anything to do with you. You saved me at Clive's. I froze up, and... you helped me out."

Kid blinked.

"Well, thank you. I owe you one."

Luke made a fist and held it out, waiting to see what she would do. She just stared at it, unmoving. Luke cleared his throat and dropped his hand. "I guess this is where we part ways. I asked Allison to come with me, but, uh... I don't think that's going to happen. Will you take care of her?"

Kid cocked her head one way and then the other. She reached up and grabbed his face between her hands and moved his head up and down in a nod.

"Something tells me Allison doesn't know about this cool trick of yours."

Her hands fell into her lap, and she turned away from him, staring into space.

"Well, your secret is safe with me."

Allison had returned to the front door, peering out, looking for them. Luke carried Kid to the house and handed her over to a grateful Allison, who wrapped her arms around her and buried her face in her hair. After a minute she looked up at Luke.

"Thank you. Not for carrying her. For rescuing us. Me. Clive cheated, but you did it. You made the throw. You won the game."

Luke was uncomfortable. He didn't much feel like he'd won anything, even if he had made the throw. Nobody had, least of all Allison. She was a mess, on the inside and the outside. He wanted to talk to her and make sure she was okay, but there wasn't any time.

"I guess I'll see you around," Luke said. He wanted to kick himself for making a joke, even if it wasn't much of one.

She gave him a half smile, her eyes tinged red as if she'd been crying or had been struggling not to. "You never know."

"Not too late to come with me."

"It is, though. It was too late before I ever met you. I get that now," she said.

Luke started to ask what she meant when Will burst into the living room in a tornado of activity. "They're gonna remember where they nabbed us. Won't take a rocket scientist for them to figure on coming back here. You two wanna hurry up?"

Will was carrying his and Al's packs; he breezed past them to the front door, where he paused. He threw something at Luke, which he caught. They were his car keys. "Good news, Doc. We don't need to steal your car anymore. Don't say I never did anything for ya. Let's go, Al."

The screen door banged behind him.

"Are you going to join the army?" Allison asked.

"I think so," Luke said. He rubbed Kid's back and patted her once as another goodbye.

"Well, don't die, you hear? Especially for something dumb."

He gave her a mock salute. "Will do."

A small smile played at her lips. "Goodbye, Luke."

"Goodbye, Allison."

Neither of them moved. Luke tried to think of something clever to say, something that would make her not forget him, maybe even make her draw comparisons to Luke the next time she met a guy. When nothing came to mind, he was considering kissing her goodbye when the horn began blaring in the truck, making them both jump.

She rolled her eyes and walked away from him, yelling out to Will. "Calm down, Will. We're coming!"

Luke watched them drive away. Afterwards he found Georgie—unhurt but skittish—and coaxed him into the car. He was halfway down the driveway when he remembered his cell phone and slammed on the brakes and rummaged in his backpack, looking for it. Instead, he pulled out a piece of paper where the phone used to be.

Doc, text me for the latest deals on all the hottest pre-owned vehicles. —Will

Dave was eleven and a half hours into a twelve-hour shift when the pickup truck rolled up and parked in front of pump number five. A girl jumped out of the passenger seat, crossed the lot briskly, and yanked the door open harder than necessary—the bell above the door screamed about it. She snatched up the sign his boss had hung on the glass about Biters not being welcome on the premises. Standing three feet from the counter, covered in what looked like blood from head to toe, she tore the sign up in front of him and sprinkled the pieces over the floor, her eyes daring him to say something about it.

Dave recognized her immediately. She was the girl from the last video feed before it went off the air. He wondered if she still had the bone that she'd used to stab that guy in the eye. He debated asking for her autograph.

She stepped forward. "I have had a terrible day. On top of that, we just stole a truck with no gas. I need fifty dollars on pump five."

"Do you have a—"

She pointed a gun at his face. "Ask me for a ration card. I dare you."

"I was, uh—going to mention that if you buy two bottles of water, you get a third free."

"Oh." She lowered the gun and put seventy dollars on the counter. "Sold. Grab 'em for me, would ya?"

Dave moved down to the end of the counter, careful to keep his hands where she could see them, and grabbed three bottles of water. He went back to his register and quickly shoved them into a plastic bag.

"You don't have paper?"

"Um, no."

"Plastic is bad for the environment." She peered at his name tag. "Dave."

"I'll mention it to the owner."

She twisted her mouth up and blew at the hair hanging in her eyes. She muttered something that sounded like "Guess we just don't care about the trees and the grass no more."

Dave rang up her waters and approved the pump on number five. He handed over the change with shaking hands. The blood on her hands was drying, and flakes fell off when he set the money in her palm.

"Hey, Dave. Is that your phone?" she asked.

Dave had left it on in case it started streaming again. The words under the video box said, "Clive's Carnival of Carnivorous Delights." He hoped she hadn't noticed that part and resisted the urge to flip it over, which would just call further attention to his guilt. "Yeah," he admitted.

She shoved the bills into her pocket, tossed crimson-smudged coins into the "take a penny, leave a penny" cup, and then leaned forward, resting her elbows on the counter. The blood on her clothes smeared across the faux-wood top. She had a wild look in her eyes that said she was as likely to gut him in the middle of the store as she was to casually lecture him about the effects of plastic on the environment.

"I'm gonna need a couple more things from you."

Dave gulped. "What's that?"

The gun was still in her hand. She looked at him, and then at the gun, and then back at him.

"The key to the restroom. And then we're gonna have us a chat about your taste in entertainment, sugar."

Season Two

S eason Two is coming to eBook and paperback on August 1, 2022. You can pre-order your copy today by visiting Naomi Ault's website.

Can't wait for more? Continue reading right now on Kindle Vella by scanning the QR code below, or typing ReadChew.Live into any web browser and starting with Episode Nineteen.

To sign up for extended scenes, contests, and bonus content, please visit Naomi's website at https://www.naomiault.com

Acknowledgments

It takes a village to plot, write, edit, cover, proofread, beta read, and format a book to get it ready for sale. My village is outstanding and extremely generous with their time. I could fill another book with the names of every person I've crossed paths with who has lent me their expertise, but I need to single out the following:

Jim for being my first and biggest fan.

Dakota and Jonathon for listening to Mom ramble about zombies at the oddest times.

Nat for being my very first beta reader.

Jason C. for being my first reader.

Nia Quinn for wrangling my scribbles into prose worth reading. I try my best to invent new grammar rules, but she never lets me get away with it.

Donika Mishineva for risking nightmares in order to produce outstanding cover art.

My fellow authors and friends from The Wordsmiths and the Kindle Vella Horror Authors Group.

Thank you all.

About the Author

Naomi Ault, the author of Chew and Discarded Objects of the Apocalypse, lives in Ohio with her husband, two children, and a border collie—who is also not known for playing sit.

Also by Naomi Ault

Chew
<u>Season Two</u> - Available on Kindle Vella - www.ReadChew.Live
Also available on eBook and paperback on August 1, 2022
<u>Season Three</u> - Available on Kindle Vella - www.ReadChew.Live

Discarded Objects of the Apocalypse Series
<u>Season One</u>: Alice Kane Must Die - Available on Kindle Vella -
www.AliceKaneMustDie.Live

Coming Fall 2022
Make Me a Dragon